T0369163

A COLD AS ICE

RALPH MOTLEY JR.

iUniverse®

COLD AS ICE

iUniverse books may be ordered through booksellers or by contacting:

iUniverse
1663 Liberty Drive
Bloomington, IN 47403
www.iuniverse.com
1-800-Authors (1-800-288-4677)

ISBN: 978-1-4917-4938-8 (sc)
ISBN: 978-1-4917-4937-1 (e)

Library of Congress Control Number: 2014919000

Printed in the United States of America.

iUniverse rev. date: 11/14/2014

Chapter 1

It had rained last night as an elderly man was walking his corgi, Mandy, in the park. He bought her two months ago, after the death of his wife of forty years.

"Hold up, Mandy! Hold up!" he screamed as he held onto the fully extended leash.

Mandy was so excited to walk that she woke him up an hour early to get on the trail in the park. He knew the walk was therapeutic for them both. As she ran ahead, something along the edge of the brushes suddenly got her attention. She snuffed the object and rolled it over with her front paws.

"What is it, girl?"

Mandy barked and wagged her tail. The old man couldn't quite make out what it was without his glasses. He reached into his fanny pack and got out his glasses, which were next to his wallet and cell phone. After donning his glasses, he knelt down for a closer look. At first, he thought it was the head of a black mannequin, but upon further inspection, he finally realized it was the real head of a black man.

"Omigod." He nervously reached back into his fanny pack and grabbed his cell phone and dialed 9-1-1.

———⟫●⟪———

The uniforms first at the scene briefed Lieutenant Zack Townes, the lead detective of the homicide division, and his partner, Sergeant Kim Patterson, who could easily pass as an Alicia Keys lookalike but taller.

"Okay, guys. Good job." Zack peered around at all the commotion. "I need this area cordoned off, and keep those media vultures at least a couple yards from the yellow tape. Don't tell them shit."

"All right, L.T."

Zack watched the medical examiner, Ken Banks, approach. Ken, twenty-five years old, was slim for his six-foot frame, and he wore glasses. As a medical examiner investigator, Zack found him to be very thorough.

Zack walked up and shook his hand. "Head's over there."

Ken grunted and pulled out his Nikon to video the scene. As Ken panned, Zack heard someone call out, "We found the rest of the body."

Every cop on the scene seemingly headed in the direction of the voice.

"Expand the perimeter!" Zack barked. "We don't need to contaminate the crime scene more than what it is right now."

Along a small slope next to a briar patch, a few feet from the railroad tracks, was a black tarp.

The uniform pointed. "There's the rest of his remains."

Zack slipped on a pair of gloves and lifted up the end of the tarp to get a peek. Kim peered over his shoulder. Zack wrinkled his nose. The smell of death wasn't something one got used to. He dropped the tarp.

"Do you think he was put on the tracks?" Kim asked.

"I don't know," Zack replied.

Many questions ran through Zack's mind at the moment. But none would be answered until an autopsy was performed. When they made their way back to where the severed head was, a throng of people had gathered.

A satellite truck was set up, and a live feed was about to start. A middle-aged brunette was all dolled up for the camera as she preened herself in front of a small mirror she was holding. She cleared her voice, and then the countdown began. The detective had stepped underneath the yellow tape and prepared to address her questions.

"I am talking to Detective Townes of Tilton."

He nodded. "Yes."

"Can you tell the viewers if a dead body is beyond the yellow police tape?"

"Yes."

"Was it a homicide or not?"

"We don't know that right now."

"Was the deceased African-American?"

"Yes."

She turned to the camera. "I would like to warn my viewers that this might be graphic. So if you would like to turn down your television sets, do so."

"Was the victim beheaded?"

Jesus, if it bleeds, it leads, Zack thought.

Zack hated vultures. "No comment."

"Okay, was it by a knife or the train?"

"What part of 'no comment' are you failing to understand?"

"Did a train sever the head?"

"Christ, lady. On the six o'clock news? Really?"

"Look," she said. "I'm just trying to get a few facts."

"Then here's one for you: this interview is over." Zack walked away.

"The press has a right to know!" She called after him.

A young cop ran up to him, waving a wallet.

"Whatever happened to decorum?" Zack asked the cop.

"What did I do?" the cop responded.

"Not you." Zack thrust a finger back at the cameras. "Prime time news over there."

The youngster looked back. "Oh, yeah. Them." He straightened his uniform.

Zack sighed. "What have you got?"

The cop switched his gaze from the cameras back to Zack. He held up the wallet. "I believe this is the vic's driver's license. I found it a couple feet from the tarp."

Zack studied it for a moment, reading the driver's license. Roger Tuck, 135 Caesar's Condominium. He turned to the officer. "Thanks."

By now, Kim had sidled up to his side. "Our vic has a name. Mr. Roger Tuck." Zack passed the driver's license to her.

"Do you know any Tucks?" she asked.

"No, not right offhand."

"At least we got his address. We'll start from there."

Chapter 2

Early the next morning, the landlady let Zack and Kim into Tuck's apartment. Zack thanked her, and she left. The furniture looked expensive and smelled new. On a glass table in front of the black leather sofa were several empty bottles of Moët and Corona. Next to them were four thin cigars, a small mound of cocaine, and an open box with one slice of pizza from Papa John's.

"Damn," Zack said. "Ol' mister Tuck likes to party."

Kim said, "I guess the stash of weed is for those cigars to be used as blunts. And he liked to snort, too."

"Cigars as blunts? That's a bit fancy, don't you think?"

"Depends on how you are," Kim replied.

Zack shrugged. "As kids, we just used rolling paper."

"You smoked weed?" Kim raised her eyebrow in mock surprise. "Not mister policeman."

"Don't even go there." He laughed. "I bet you did, too."

They were taking in their surroundings as they moved across the living quarters. "Yeah, that was the in thing to do at that time, I suppose," Kim said.

Zack headed for the kitchen, just off the living room, and checked the sink. There were a few plates with half-eaten slices of pizza on the kitchen counter and in the sink, as if someone were in a rush. Then he searched the cabinets. It was nearly empty except for a couple packets of Oodles of Noodles, Vienna sausages, potted meat, and crackers. Mr. Tuck wasn't too much on cooking. He peered into the trash can. Nothing.

Kim checked out the master bedroom. The huge oak bed was unmade, as a black satin sheet hung halfway on the floor. Beside the bed surrounded by empty bottles of JD and Fireball was an old-fashioned answering machine. Beneath a dusting of coke, Kim could see a blinking red light. It seemed someone had left Mr. Tuck a message. She pulled out some latex gloves from her back pocket, donned them, and pushed the button.

"Mr. Tuck," said an angry voice with a heavy Latino accent, "you ass is mines! Where my shipment, man? I will git you. Yes, I will!"

When he finished, Kim pushed the button again.

A young female voice whispered, "Roger, Roger, please. Where are you, baby? I'm worried about you, sweetie. I hope you're okay."

That was the end of the messages.

"Zack!"

He entered the bedroom. "What's up?"

Kim hit the rewind button. "Check this out." She pressed play.

Zack listened intently to both recordings. He chuckled. "Sounds promising. We have a direct threat and a scared girlfriend. You think they're connected?"

"Hard to say," Kim replied. "With all the booze and blow, I'd say Mr. Tuck was a very naughty boy. Probably made several enemies."

Zack nodded. "Maybe even a spurned lover."

"You don't think," Kim said. "I mean, she sounds so young."

Zack shrugged. "You never know."

Kim let it drop. She still had some hope that not everyone was bad. "Let's see what the landlady knows."

The landlady couldn't identify the Hispanic voice, but she said the young lady was Audrey Scott, a college student from a rough area. She went to school with the landlady's daughter, but something got between them.

Chapter 3

Zack and Kim pulled up to an abandoned eighteen-wheeler on I-95. A K-9 unit sat near the trailer. The dog was already out, barking at the sealed back door. They got out and approached the K-9 officer.

Zack asked, "What do you have?"

"Drugs, Detective Townes," the K-9 officer replied.

"Where?"

"Inside the trailer."

"I don't see it." Zack stared at the metal tag. "Somebody get me some bolt cutters so I can pop this damn tag off."

The dog came over and brushed against Zack's leg. He rubbed its head and coat, and the German shepherd wagged his tail.

"Here you go, Detective." The K-9 officer passed him the bolt cutters and motioned for the dog to move.

The detective snapped the metal tag, flipped the latch, and pulled up the door. Small bundles of brown paper wrapped in plastic rolled out the trailer and onto the ground.

"I believe we hit the mother lode."

Much to Zack's chagrin, once word got out about the truckload of drugs, top brass from the chief down to the shift supervisors were on the scene, mugging for the television camera. The mayor was out of town, but his assistant, Tad, was front and center.

Once the confiscated trailer load of drugs was taken to the station, every ounce was processed by weight and logged into the computer. The estimated street value of the many kilos of cocaine and marijuana was estimated to be nearly $10 million. Needless to say, the evidence locker area where the illicit drugs were stashed was heavily guarded. An officer was posted around the clock, and a camera was mounted as insurance.

Chapter 4

Big Nasty and Mayor Brownlow had planned a secret meeting a hundred miles from Tilton in the Blue Ridge Mountains. The remote area was nearly a quarter mile high. They had met there on a couple occasions. Nasty wasn't too crazy about the place because he had to hike about a half mile after they had parked. The chosen spot was in front of a six-foot, open cave that disappeared into the side of a mountain.

Nasty had gotten there early. He was sitting on a huge log, getting his breath. Brownlow approached. Nasty couldn't figure out how a chump that looked like a Danny DeVito impersonator could score so many women.

Sure, the guy was smooth, but fuck, what were these bitches? Blind?

When Brownlow saw Nasty, he said, "My main man."

They bear-hugged. Nasty leaned forward as he never got up from the log. Strictly about business, Nasty reached down and picked up the leather knapsack full of money.

"This is another hundred grand, Ray. So I can carry on with our agreement." Nasty handed over the money.

Brownlow's eyes got wider as he opened up the flap and gazed at the stacks of money with bands across them. "No problem. No problem, mon," Brownlow said in a weak Jamaican accent.

Nasty scowled. *Prick.*

Brownlow sniffed the cash. "Ah, the sweet smell of money."

Nasty didn't care for his antics. He stood upright and towered over the little man. "So is we straight, man, or what?"

Brownlow stared up at him. Fear spread across his face. "Yes, we are straight. I told you I will have my men on the job."

"Let's hope so. 'Cause I will be your worst nightmare."

Chapter 5

Zack had chosen an open-air deli downtown called Sandra's Subs. It was a mild July afternoon. He and Kim had chosen a shaded area over in a corner with a wooden table. A light breeze had kicked up. This was the only smoking section. Zack shook out a Newport from the pack and lit it.

"So what do you think?"

"Well, it seems to me he was supposed to be transporting that load somewhere on the East Coast, probably New York City."

"Here's what I believe." Zack snubbed out his Newport in an ashtray. "Mr. Tuck had picked up his shipment in El Paso. He probably could be connected to a Mexican drug cartel in some capacity. And he was holding out on them. He had moved to Virginia, trying to get as far away as possible from where he was supposed to go. He could have wanted to make Virginia his home in the future because it was the route he traveled. He probably loved the lifestyle that drugs provided and was looking to break away from the cartel."

"What about the girl?" Kim asked.

"Well …" Zack sighed, pulled out another cigarette, and lit it. "When you have expensive things, women seem to come out of the woodwork."

"C'mon, Zack," Kim said. "That's not fair. It's a terrible generalization."

"Okay, let me say it like this. Almost every successful athlete, entertainer, or even drug dealer always has the prettiest or sexiest woman on his arm."

"Well …" Kim sipped from her drink. "I guess there's a kernel of truth to what you are saying."

Ten minutes later, they left Sandra's to pay a visit to Ms. Scott. Ms. Scott lived in the blighted, old section of the town. Every house on her street was in disrepair and close to collapsing. When Zack rapped on the door, a brown-skinned young lady of twenty, who was very pretty and very pregnant, opened the door.

Zack towered over her, taking up most of the door frame.

Audrey peeked around him and saw the squad car. "Anything wrong, Officer?"

"I'm Detective Townes, and that's my partner, Sergeant Patterson. May we come in?"

"Yeah."

Surprisingly, the living room was very clean and tidy, but the furniture was dated.

"Why were you trying to get in contact with Mr. Tuck the other day?" Zack asked.

"Is anything wrong, Officer?" she asked again.

"Yes. He's dead."

Ms. Scott began to sob and sway. "Oh my God. Oh my God."

Kim quickly went around her to keep her from hitting the floor. Kim caught her and moved her to the couch. Ms. Scott clasped her hands on her face and sobbed for five minutes straight. The tears slowed down as she tried to gain her composure.

When she seemed more collected, Zack asked, "Were you guys dating?"

"Yes." She pulled at her shirtsleeve and stared at the floor. "We have matching Cupid tattoos."

"How long?"

"About a year. This is his baby. I'm due at any time."

"Did you know what kind of business he was in?"

"No, but he traveled a lot."

"Was he good to you?"

She dabbed at her eyes with a tissue. "What do you mean?"

"Treat you with respect."

"Absolutely. He wasn't anything like other guys I've dated in the past. They were abusive and childish. Boys pretending to be all hard but not men."

"Did he say anything about someone being after him?"

She paused as if weighing the question. "Yeah, he said some Mexicans were out to get him. He told me, if he could ever straighten things out with them, he would take care of me and our baby."

Zack looked over at Kim and gave her that I-told-you-so look. "How long did he have the condo?"

"Not long. About four months."

Zack's cell rang. He pulled it out of his pocket and looked at the screen. It was the medical examiner. Zack thanked her. He was sorry for her loss and the baby. He left his card.

And he and Kim were gone.

Chapter 6

Men are so weak, she thought to herself, *especially when it comes to shapely, pretty women clad in a hot outfit.*

Strutting down a side street from the business district in Tilton and wearing a light blue blouse with no bra, a navy miniskirt, and a pair of white pumps while holding tight to her purse certainly got the attention of several drivers passing by. The men who passed her whistled, while the women turned their noses up in disgust or jealousy.

And when she made it to the curb, a fifty-something, white male driving a red Corvette screamed, "Need a ride, ma'am?"

She paused for a beat, weighing his question. "Sure." She opened the door and hopped in.

The driver sped down the street and, about a mile down the road, took a ramp to the highway.

He extended his hand as he kept his eyes on the road. "My name is Kyle."

She shook his hand. "My name is Caitlyn. I'm new to the area." Caitlyn wasn't her real name, but it was her first time in Tilton. She had arrived in town less than a week ago.

"Want to go to my place and have a little fun?"

She smirked. "What's your idea of fun?"

"You know." He shrugged. "A couple drinks and whatever happens from there happens. You drink, don't you?"

"Absolutely."

"Great."

Twenty minutes later, Kyle arrived at his Colonial-style home in the suburbs. It was a very wooded area. His nearest neighbor was at least a half-mile away. He stopped in front of the garage and pushed a remote on his key chain. The garage door went up. He pulled in, he hit the button, and the door closed behind them. Everything was tidy and neat. A few shelves held bottles of paint and motor oil.

Caitlyn took in her surroundings as she stared out the car window. He cut the engine and rushed out of the driver side to open the door for her. And when she turned to get out, he got an eyeful of her crotch. She was wearing a white thong. She caught him watching. A mix of pleasure and contempt coursed through her veins. Men were some strange beings, she always thought, especially after the incident as a little girl. She tried her best to suppress the ugly feeling that kept bubbling up inside her.

Enjoy the moment. Enjoy the moment, a chant she ran through her mind echoed.

Caitlyn and Kyle walked through the door and entered a hallway that led to the kitchen.

"You have a nice home," Caitlyn said. "Looks like it has a lady's touch. Don't tell me you're married."

"No, no. Used to be though." He threw his keys on the counter. He brushed up against her, grabbed her by the waist, and lightly tapped her tush. She tensed up a little. He let her go and walked into the kitchen. "So what would you like to drink? Beer, wine, or liquor?"

"Got any Grey Goose?"

"Yeah, for sure." He laughed. "My favorite. You want it straight or mixed?"

"Straight."

He poured them two glasses of Grey Goose and led Caitlyn to the living room. They took a seat on a brown sectional that sat in front of a glass table. A sixty-two-inch plasma television hung on the opposite wall.

Kyle grabbed the TV remote and clicked it on. "Anything in particular you want to watch?"

"Not really. But I do watch the Lifetime Channel sometimes."

"Okay." He switched the station to Lifetime and then took a long swallow, almost finishing his glass.

Silence ensued. Kyle tried to make eye contact with her, but she averted her eyes by staring up at the TV. He then reached over and grabbed her right thigh.

She quickly removed his hand. "Not now, mister."

He laughed and then reached up and cupped her right breast. She slapped his hand.

Kyle said, "If not now, when?"

"What's the rush?" Caitlyn asked.

With a tinge of anger in his voice, Kyle asked, "What the hell you think we're here for? If I wanted to watch soap operas all day, I could have done that by myself."

"You got the wrong gal, mister."

"What do you mean?" Kyle was getting angrier by the second. "I asked if you wanted to have some fun."

"Watching soaps is fun," Caitlyn said.

"Don't play stupid." Kyle jumped up and went back to pour himself another glass of Grey Goose.

Meanwhile, Caitlyn was feeling nervous and excited. Men always showed anger when they didn't get what they wanted. Kyle was no different.

When he was seated back on the couch, Kyle sat even closer to her and tried to make an even bolder move. He wanted to kiss her. She instinctively turned her head in disgust. With his temper rising, he attacked her, pouncing on her like a lion on its prey on the safari.

"Look here, you whore, you trying to play hard to get?" He overpowered her as he climbed on top.

"Stop! Stop, you bastard!"

He slapped her, and as she kept resisting, then he punched her hard several times in the face, knocking her semiconscious. By now, Caitlyn was on the floor. Kyle ripped off her thong, and he was raping her. Caitlyn tried desperately to shake away the cobwebs from the devastating punches.

Kyle never let up. He kept screwing her, the whole time saying, "Yeah, baby. That feels real good."

Slightly disoriented and steady getting her bearings, Caitlyn jogged her mind to what was going on. And once she did, she pretended she was still knocked out, squeezing her eyes like they were shut and watching her assailant assault her as he continually forced himself inside of her body. It really pissed her off and she felt anger surge through her veins.

Next, she peered around for her purse. It was next to her on the floor. As Kyle reached his climax and let out a sound of ecstasy, the next sound was that of horror because, no sooner had he pulled out his penis, than Caitlyn whacked off his manhood in one swipe.

"Oh shit!" he screamed in agony. "I'm going to die!"

"You're damn right." Caitlyn scrambled to her feet. "How does it feel now, asshole?"

"Help! Help me."

She leaned down and slit his throat. She stood over him for a bit with a look of satisfaction on her face. Then she began to clean off the straight razor. She found a bottle of Clorox in the pantry and wiped down everything she touched from inside the house to the Corvette that brought her there. Then she hiked through the woods and back toward the downtown.

Caitlyn was exhausted when she got back to her apartment and wearily flopped across the bed, face-down. Then she rolled over, looked at her bloody clothes, and hoped nobody saw her on the way to her place. *Job well done*, she thought to herself.

It was as if two people lived inside of her. *Sybil*, the psycho with multiple personalities, was her favorite movie. But Caitlyn knew she had two personalities, one good one and the bad one that her tormentors helped create when she was savagely raped as a little girl.

————⟫●⟪————

Caitlyn's mother, Bonita Cortez, had worked countless dead-end jobs. She and Caitlyn were seemingly always moving from one residence to another, in part because Bonita rarely paid her rent like she should. Whenever she got a place for her and her daughter, she would always pay up front, like the deposit and the first three months, but hardly ever paid more because her money went into drugs and alcohol. And while Bonita was high, several of her lovers over the years would lust after her daughter, Caitlyn.

Caitlyn had warned Bonita when she was sober that the men were making gestures and making her feel uncomfortable, as they would stare at her. But being a self-absorbed, alcoholic, junkie whore, Bonita just dismissed what Caitlyn was saying. In no time, her mother's different lovers had raped her multiple times. When the first rape happened, something in Caitlyn died. She had lost her innocence. She wanted to report it to her teachers at her school, but her mother's lack of concern disillusioned her so much that she felt the school would react the same way. So she did nothing.

But in a rather bizarre way, she vowed to herself that she would get the bastards back in her own way some day. Right now, she would say like an internal chant, *I'm a child, but when I get older, they will pay. So this is the hand I was dealt. I just need to stay in survival mode in order to live.*

Over the next couple years, Caitlyn blossomed into a beautiful, shapely princess. Some thought she was of Italian or Greek descent because of her tan complexion with long, black, flowing hair. Most men swooned at her beauty. The rare moments when Bonita was sober, she just scoffed at all the attention her daughter received about her looks and body.

In fits of jealousy, she would say, "You little bitch, you ain't all that. Hell, I was just as pretty when I was your age. Plus, beauty doesn't last forever."

Bonita would especially condemn Caitlyn when she would comb her hair while staring into the mirror on the bureau.

Under her breath, Caitlyn would say, "Yeah, drugs, alcohol, and your men robbed you of your former life. Don't blame me."

Chapter 7

Kim and Zack visited the office of the medical examiner, Dr. Cynthia Powell. She had replaced Dr. Williams, who had been the medical examiner for forty-plus years. He was very successful, respected, and well-liked. Dr. Powell knew she had some huge shoes to fill. The forty-something, caramel-skinned forensic pathologist stood nearly six feet.

She's average-looking. Nothing special, Kim thought.

She was wearing her green scrubs while sitting at her desk listening to some old R&B, The Temptations, to be exact. The lead singer's voice emanated from a small CD player on the floor. She was putting the finishing touches on her autopsy report. As they entered, Kim heard a beeping sound. The medical examiner turned toward the sound and got up from her desk.

"What was that?" Kim asked.

Dr. Powell chuckled. "That's my warning system. I installed a motion-activated sensor at the entrance. I don't like surprises."

They shook the doctor's hand and followed her over to the stainless steel autopsy table.

"So, what do you think happened to Mr. Tuck?" Zack asked.

"Well ..." She sighed. "Whoever did this was extremely mad."

A soiled, bloodstained white sheet covered the body. There was about a foot-long gap under the bloody sheet, where the detached head was separated from the rest of the body. The medical examiner slowly pulled back the top of the sheet, exposing the severed head. It was resting on its side. The cops' gazes traveled down past the neck area to the Cupid tattoo on his shoulder.

Kim whispered, nudging Zack. "There's the tat of Cupid that Audrey talked about."

Dr. Powell had donned a pair of green latex gloves as she had begun to touch and move the head. "See those cut marks at the base of the skull?"

They nodded.

"Someone had a sharp object, possibly a kitchen knife. The perp used a cutting motion as he sawed off his head."

"So it wasn't from the train?" Kim asked. "Because he wasn't that far from it."

"No," Dr. Powell said. "The pressure from the train would have squeezed off his head. Just like you might do from a wad of dough when making homemade bread. Those are saw and hacking marks."

The cops moved in to get a closer look.

"Yeah, yeah. I see what you are talking about," Zack said. "It's like watching a butcher sectioning off meat from a slab."

"Yes, that's another way of putting it, Detective."

"Was he alive when all that cutting happened?" Kim asked.

"No. I don't think so."

The medical examiner turned the head so they could see the top of it. And she then parted the matted coarse hair and showed them the small bullet hole. "He was shot first with a small caliber gun. Then after that, I believe he was decapitated."

"Were you able to get the bullet out?" Zack inquired.

"Yes. I have it in an envelope on my desk. I'll give it to you before you all leave."

"So, Doc, how long had he been dead?" Kim asked.

"With the liver test, the stage of rigor, and contents in his stomach, I'd say seven to eight hours."

"All right, Dr. Powell. Thanks," Zack said. "And welcome to Tilton."

She nodded, smiled, shook both of their hands, and then handed over the white envelope with the bullet in it.

Chapter 8

As he shook Mr. Pruitt's hand, Zack realized that all the publicity might have actually turned up a lead. The sixty-something railway worker said he wanted to come by because he saw something, and the news had jogged his memory. Zack motioned for Mr. Pruitt to have a seat. Mr. Pruitt sat down and took off his cap, exposing his bald head.

Kim took out a pad. "So, Mr. Pruitt, what did you see some weeks back?"

Mr. Pruitt fidgeted with his ball cap. "Well, I'm an engineer for Norfolk Southern, and that night, we weren't steaming that fast back to our destination. I guess we were moving about twenty."

Zack jumped in. "Around what time was that, sir?"

"It was midnight. Full moon. Haven't been late in thirty years. 'Cept to dinner." He turned to Kim and winked. "With the missus cooking, you'd be late, too." He let out a little laugh. "As we—me and my crew—traveled down the tracks, up ahead was a beam of light. Frank said it was aliens, but that durn fool watches too many movies. I said it was probably some kids trying to shoot across the rails and beat the train. So I pulled on the whistle to scare them. But as we approached the beam of light, I noticed it wasn't moving. It was headlights from one of them SUVs, and about five or six Mexicans were beating this black guy to a pulp. He was in front of the SUV on his knees. They just kept punching and kicking him. Six to one. That wasn't a fight. It was a beating. Probably gangs."

"Did they ever look up at the train?" Zack asked.

"No, they never did. They were too busy beating up that black feller."

Zack asked, "Are you sure they were Hispanic?"

"They were Mexicans for sure. My brother has a huge tobacco farm, and he gets a bunch of them during the summer. So I kind of know how they look."

"Did you recognize any from the farm?" Kim asked.

"No, no. The ones that work for my brother, they just like to work and occasionally drink a little too much. They work hard and send money back home to their families."

Zack hopped back on Kim's line of questioning. "What makes you so sure that it wasn't your brother's workers?"

"Well, I might be wrong. It could be them. You just never know."

"What's your brother's name?"

"Sammy Pruitt."

"Where's his tobacco farm?"

"Out on the edge of town."

"Do his workers stay until the harvesting of the crop, or do they stay year-round?"

"I don't really know, but I do see them in the off season."

"Could you describe your brother?"

Hesitating and with a pleading tone, Mr. Pruitt said, "I didn't mean to put pressure on my baby brother. I was just doing my citizen's duty."

"We understand. And we appreciate that." Kim assured him.

"Can I leave after I answer your last questions?"

They nodded yes.

"He's five years younger. Not quite so good looking, though Ma might tell ya different. About same height." Mr. Pruitt patted his gut. "And we both been putting on a few pounds."

"Hair color?" Zack asked.

Mr. Pruitt ran his hand over his bald head. "Same as mine. Dad's fault."

Chapter 9

Zack drove out to the Pruitt farm just outside Tilton. The blacktop service road gave way to a rocky dirt road. As the squad car sped down the dirt road, a cloud of dust trailed behind the car. He passed several tobacco barns, a couple small frame houses, and a group of Mexicans working in the field, heading on his way toward a mound where a large, white house was situated.

Zack got out of the car and headed for a small flight of stairs attached to a wraparound porch. Before he could scale the short stairs, a slightly overweight white male in his fifties met him. Zack immediately noticed the striking resemblance to his brother Karl. After flashing his badge and introducing himself, Zack asked if they could talk.

"Sure," Sammy said. "Want to talk on the porch? It's such a beautiful sunny day."

"Of course."

They took a seat in two straw rocking chairs.

"Would you like something to drink?"

"No," Zack said. "But thanks."

"So, why are you here, Detective?"

"There was a murder a few weeks ago, and your brother said he saw a group of Mexicans beating up a black man."

Mr. Pruitt coughed. "I don't think any of my workers would do something like that."

The cough felt suspicious. *Is Mr. Pruitt hiding something? Maybe. Or it could just be seasonal allergies.* Zack hated to read too much into it, so he left it on the back burner for now.

From his vantage point, Zack could see the Mexican workers across the field at a good distance. Several of the males would look up nervously toward them as they spoke.

Mr. Pruitt continued. "My workers aren't the only Mexican workers around here."

"I understand you are looking out for them."

"Yeah. I couldn't run this farm if it weren't for them."

"I get that," Zack said. "So do you get the same workers each year?"

"Yes, pretty much." Mr. Pruitt paused for a few seconds. "I let a couple families live in those small houses on my property year-round. They are excellent workers. Every once in a while, a few might drink too much, especially on Cinco de Mayo. But for the most part, they don't cause any trouble."

"So the ones who are living in your houses are legal?"

Mr. Pruitt coughed again. "I didn't ask for any birth certificates, but I assume they are. You press too hard, and you're liable to scare them off, what with all this immigration stuff going on today." A pensive look crossed his face. "You're not going to bust me for this. I need them to work the farm."

"I'm not from immigration." Zack saw some possible leverage, so he decided to use it. "You don't look like the type that would lie. I see no reason to stir up trouble for you. I'm just looking for some info on a homicide."

Mr. Pruitt's shoulders relaxed, and he settled back into the chair.

"Are there any new workers that you don't know that much about and perhaps could be capable of such an act?" Zack asked.

Mr. Pruitt thought about the question. "Well, the first house you passed is my newest workers. The guys been working for me for about three weeks. It's about four of them. They're young, maybe twenties."

"Why them?"

"They don't seem to be in a rush to work, not like the other ones."

"So they're lazy."

"I'm not racist or anything. Most of these guys are hardworking family men."

"But the new ones are lazy?"

"Yeah, you can say that. Fixing to fire them after the season, of course."

"Where are they now?"

Mr. Pruitt stood up and peered out across the field. "I don't know. I thought I saw them working out there somewhere."

"What type of vehicle were they driving when they asked to work for you?"

Mr. Pruitt waggled a finger. "Now that's the strangest damn thing. It was rather nice, a black, fancy SUV. Might even have been one of those Jap cars. A Lexus or something."

Zack's heart began to race. A smile crept across his face. "Did they give you their names?"

"Is it them?"

"Possibly. The perps were driving a black SUV."

"Okay, names and description. All probably in twenties."

"Jose is short, about five-two and fat. Juan is tall, about six feet and slim. And Rafa was the leader of the three. He's solid, like he lifted weights. He was about five-ten and spoke the best English."

That was odd. Given the number of migrant workers and the fact these guys were new, Mr. Pruitt either had a photographic memory or a reason to remember them. Zack decided to put that on the back burner, too. It was getting crowded back there.

Zack whipped out his notepad and jotted down the information. "Do you know their license plate number?"

"Nope."

So much for a photographic memory.

"Are they Texas tags?"

"Yep, but most of them have Texas plates."

Zack thanked Mr. Pruitt and decided to put a BOLO out on the vehicle. He might get lucky with the workers. As he drove away from the farm, he also thought he might need to pay some special attention to Mr. Pruitt. The old man was hiding something. He felt sure of that.

Chapter 10

Big Nasty was nicknamed as such because of his girth, attitude, and prowess in bed with the women. Standing five-ten and weighing three fifty, he was a huge man with a hair-trigger temper. Being well-endowed made him popular with the ladies.

At one time, some twenty years ago, before all the weight gain, Nasty was a handsome young man. According to some of his lady friends, he resembled Billy Dee Williams with a Jheri curl. Nasty wasn't a shrinking violet about how good he was in bed. He had a saying once. They, his women, got of piece of the rock, and they always came back for more.

But as time passed, he didn't care too much about his appearance. He just let himself go, pigging out at all the buffets across town. Outside of sex and making money, little else mattered in his world. And when he started dealing drugs, he was busted a time a two. But his time in prison was like a training ground for how not to get caught selling drugs. Within a year after serving his last prison sentence, Nasty had amassed a small fortune from the drug trade. He truly considered himself a legit businessman.

"Shit, I pay my taxes on my businesses," he would say. "I have every right to the American dream as the next guy."

He knew full well his drug money was funneled through his strip clubs and escort services. He also had another answer for that, too. He would often say to his lackeys, "Tell me any rich person who got rich with clean hands. They have done some crooked stuff to get on their feet, and now some of them are so-called good, upstanding citizens. Man, give me a damn break. I might have been born at night, but not last night. Y'all know that saying."

Nasty knew he had to tread lightly because he knew he was still on the cops' radar.

Because he was such big man, Nasty had a gait that was more like a wobble. And when he smiled, every other tooth was missing. It changed his speech pattern. He couldn't pronounce certain words proper. It didn't matter because he was semi-illiterate, as he quit school in the fifth grade.

Nasty's reputation grew within the underworld. He befriended Mafia types and other shysters in New York City, Richmond, and Miami. He surrounded himself with a tight-knit band of goons he called his boys or crew. Their job was to take orders from him and be his bodyguards around the clock. But they were more like flunkeys than anything else. They were afraid of him.

A late addition to the crew was a dwarf called Rat, so named became of his small size, his slightly longish face with sharp, pointy teeth, and a straggly mustache that looked like whiskers.

It was rather strange how Nasty and his boys met Rat. Last year during the holidays, they were strolling past a Christmas display in a huge storefront with Santa Claus and his helpers. And Rat stood motionless, decked out in his red outfit.

"Is that a mannequin?" Nasty asked one of his boys.

"Hell yeah." Two Bit Tony said emphatically.

Rat stood next to the sleigh with a bag of toys pouring out, and around him were four other mannequins the same height as him. He was still not blinking or moving as Nasty and his group drew near the window to inspect closer.

"Boo!" Rat hollered.

They all ran into each other, getting the hell out of the way. All except Nasty. He just stood there smiling. Realizing they'd been had, he laughed like crazy as the entered the retail store.

Even though he liked scaring people, Rat was tired of the little gig. So he marched from the display window, right toward the cashier where Nasty and the boys were paying for a few items.

Nasty asked the cashier, staring down at Rat. "How much for Santa's helper?"

The female cashier looked down at Rat with a wry smile. "Seeing how he ain't prime rib, I'd say ten cents a pound."

"Ten cents a pound?" Rat looked up at the cashier. "At that rate, you'd go broke buying just what's in my pants."

"Hardly, sweetie," the cashier said. "I have a nickel in my pocket, and I'd expect some change."

Nasty and his crew laughed.

Then Rat ripped off his pointy red hat with a white ball on top. "I'm tired of being a damn clown for this minimum-wage Christmas crap."

A thought crossed Nasty's mind. "Hey, little man. Forget that ho. Want to hang with us?"

Rat looked at the cashier, whose smile had evaporated under the "ho" comment. He thought about it a second, "Sure. Why not?" He tossed the hat on the counter. "Tell the boss I quit."

Chapter 11

Caitlyn had laid out a red wraparound skirt and a pink blouse on top of the bed. And just before hitting the shower, she retrieved a pair of white pumps from the closet. Ten minutes later, she exited the shower and peered at her naked body in front of a full-length mirror. She wasn't modest about her looks or body. She liked what she saw. Then she leaned in closer to get a better look at the scar under her right eye. She smashed her fist into the mirror until the rage subsided.

Think of something else. So she shifted her focus back to her shapely figure. Her peach-sized breasts were accented by a small waist that gave way to an almost perfectly round butt. She quickly got dressed and re-examined how she looked clothed.

"Stunning," she said.

Tonight, she'd kill with that getup. She chortled, and a sly smile spread across her face. Like a moth to a flame, they'd come after her under the pretext of wanting to be friends, all the while trying to get her in bed.

It was Saturday night, and she had a bar/club in mind called Miley's she wanted to check out after passing it a few times. It was located on the north side of Tilton. It catered toward the working-class or blue-collar worker. Most of the patrons were middle-aged and of all races. Caitlyn decided she would call a taxi and have the driver drop her off a block away so nobody there could see how she got there, a quirky thing she lived by.

It was nine o'clock when she stepped into the club. That was after paying her seven dollars at the door. Once inside, she paused and gave it a quick glance. The dance floor was half-full, and she saw several men's eyes concentrating on her. She smiled inside.

"Just as I thought," she said to herself.

After finding an empty booth around the dance floor, she headed for it as a Donna Summer song filled the air. Within what seemed like seconds, two guys almost ran toward her booth, asking to sit with her. She laughed in spite of herself. They both were white, middle-aged men with thinning hair. One was tall while the other one was short. She politely dismissed the short man. He shrugged his shoulders and left.

"Must be my lucky day." The tall man was wearing a white, short-sleeved shirt and Levi's. He extended his hand before sitting down. "My name is Stan. And yours?"

She shook it. "Caitlyn."

"Nice to meet you, Caitlyn." Stan settled in his seat.

A young waitress made her way to their booth. "Drinks anybody?"

"What would you like, beautiful?" Stan asked.

"Rum and coke," she replied.

"Make that two rum and cokes," Stan said.

The DJ was playing "Back that Thing Up" by the rap artist Juvenile. Some of the patrons were headed for the dance floor. Stan bobbed his head to the beat and then asked Caitlyn if she wanted to dance.

"Sure, why not?"

Stan grabbed her hand, and they danced to Juvenile's cut and two more songs before they headed back to their seats. The waitress was there, waiting to get paid as their drinks sat on the table. After Stan paid her, she went on to another table.

They drank and danced until one in the morning.

"How about if we went to my apartment and cap off the wonderful night?"

She waited just a bit. She felt a little voice urge her on, so she said, "Okay, I'm down with that."

Fifteen minutes later, they strolled into his cozy apartment. It was too nice for a single man.

"You did say you were single when we were on the dance floor, right?" she asked. "I'm not down with being jumped by some crazy ass, jealous girlfriend."

"Nah, just me. Me and you, babe," Stan said with a slur from the alcohol. "I need to pee."

Caitlyn was still clutching her purse. It gave her a sense of comfort with her gun, Taser, and straight razor inside. The straight razor almost spoke to her. *You could do it now while he's in the bathroom. Cut him off midstream.*

"Make yourself at home," Stan called, breaking her train of thought. "There's a remote. If you need some booze, the bar's in the corner."

Caitlyn went to the bar and poured herself a screwdriver. She retreated to the couch and snatched up the remote. Nothing was on Lifetime, so she kept flipping channels, flooding her mind with a series of worthless images.

Within minutes, Stan was back from using the bathroom. He flopped down on the couch beside Caitlyn. She had the remote, and she was flipping through channels.

"I believe my bed would be a better place for us to really get acquainted.

Told ya that you should have done it in the bathroom, the razor said. *Beds are so hard to clean.*

Caitlyn put down the remote, turned, and gave Stan a sexy look. She grabbed her purse. "Sounds good, lover."

They headed down the hall toward the bedroom. And when they were there, Caitlyn said, "I have an idea."

"What's that?" Stan was hurriedly taking off his shoes and unbuttoning his shirt.

"Let's play this game." She let out a little laugh. "I'm going to blindfold you, get undressed, too, and see how intimate we can get."

"I never tried this before, but it sounds good."

"It will be fun." Caitlyn assured him. "Got something I can blindfold you with?"

"Sure." Stan got up, walked over to a dresser, and pulled out a tie. "How about this?" It was red. She'd heard it called a "power tie" on one of the talk shows. She liked the irony.

"Perfect," Caitlyn said. "Sit right here on the edge of the bed while I tie your blindfold and get undressed."

"Giddy with excitement here," Stan said. "I just can't wait to make love to you." He practically tapped his feet on the floor like a little boy.

"That makes two of us." She undid her bra. Her breasts swung free. Then she grabbed Stan's hands to let him feel them.

"Nice. Just my size."

In the next moment, Caitlyn reached into her purse, and took out the .380.

No, the razor said in protest. *Let me play first.*

Not tonight, she thought. She still felt the bruises from last time. She wanted something easy this time.

Her tone turned serious. "Lay back, Stan."

"What are you going to do?" he asked nervously.

She leaned in close and whispered, "Don't worry, Stan. I don't bite. Just lie back on the bed and relax. I'm going to climb on top."

A goofy grin replaced his fear. "Oh, oh, okay."

And when he did, she pounced on top of him with gun in hand. Then she grabbed a pillow next to him. Stan tried to resist, but it was too late. Caitlyn stuffed the pillow over his face and squeezed off two rounds in succession. Stan kicked a few times.

"Dumbass," Caitlyn said with contempt.

Somewhere in the alley, she could hear a dog howling. Off in the distance, a siren pierced the night. It wasn't after her, not so soon, but someone had to have heard. She knew her razor wanted to play, but it would have to wait for a different night. She quickly gathered her things and left.

Chapter 12

Over the last year or so, Zack's life had become nothing short of a whirlwind of activity. For starters, his second divorce was finally over. In the settlement, he got his vehicles and his personal belongings, and his ex-wife got the house and furniture, just like the first divorce. Also, Zack would have to pay child support for his six-year-old son, along with visitation rights.

No sooner had that issue been addressed, than the mother of his first two children, both teenagers, passed away from ovarian cancer. After her death, he had custody of them. In addition, his current lover and partner on the force, Kim, had a seven-year-old boy, Hosea. Zack knew it would make for an interesting family unit. They had recently purchased a two-story Colonial with four bedrooms, three bathrooms, a game room in the basement, and a wraparound deck, which sat on three acres.

It will be a juggling act for sure, Zack thought. He had informed all the kids he wanted to meet them in the game room and go over some ground rules for the household.

"First and foremost," he said, to his kids in particular, "I love all of you very deeply."

Kim stood beside him and nodded. Zack glanced at his sixteen-year-old daughter, Kathy. *God, she looks just like her mother.* He found it unnerving. And like her mother always did when she didn't want to listen, Kathy rolled her eyes. He looked to his son, Johnny, for support, but Johnny showed his displeasure by folding his arms and flopping down in the chair.

Zack sighed. "This is new to all of us. But one thing I will not tolerate is disrespect for grown-ups."

Kathy bowed her head and stared at the floor.

Zack gave the floor to Kim. She cleared her throat. "I know I'm not your mother, and I don't want to pretend to be. So I can only be myself. I love you guys, and we can make this work. That's if you want it to."

Hosea sheepishly glanced over at his new family members. Zack's cell rang. He snapped it loose from its holster.

Kathy stood up. "Great family meeting, Dad. Guess I'll go to my room."

Zack held up a finger and halted her. He gazed at the display screen. It was the chief. He motioned for Kathy to sit back down. She scowled but complied. Zack stepped out of the game room onto the deck outside. Then he touched the screen to receive the call.

"Enjoy your trip to El Paso, Detective," Chief Watts said.

A wide smile appeared on Zack's face. Ever since the large stash of drugs was found in Mr. Tuck's tractor trailer, Zack had been hounding the chief about going to El Paso and trying to get to the bottom of what was going on. In the past, there had been other random checks on the interstate of semis being busted for drugs from Texas. But this one in particular was the largest by far.

"Thank you, sir," Zack said happily.

"Under one condition," the chief said. "You bring us back some valuable information that might help stop or slow down those shipments of drugs up and down the I-95 corridor, in addition to solving the Tuck murder."

"Sure thing. Absolutely," Zack said. "So how soon can I leave?"

"According to your ticket, you leave tomorrow out of Raleigh-Durham at ten in the morning."

"Again, thanks, Chief."

They hung up.

Kim was still reiterating what Zack had said earlier when he came back in the game room.

Zack picked up where she left off. "You guys are older now, so that means more responsibilities. I'm going to go over some more rules for the house. Clean your rooms, and make your beds every morning. I expect y'all to be up and ready to eat breakfast by six. Your school clothes will be laid out the night before. And when you get home from school, take off your school clothes, put on your regular clothes, and do your chores. Like cutting the lawn, taking out the trash, shaping the hedges, and keeping the inside of the house tidy, to name few. We all will pitch in.

"Next, homework is very important. After your chores, I expect you guys to do your homework. If you need my study to concentrate, use it. But so long as you keep everything like it is, which is neat and orderly. Kim and I are college graduates, so average grades aren't good enough. So give your best, and if we can help with your homework, feel free to ask us if we aren't busy.

"Lastly, she and I are gone mostly during the day. As a matter of fact, we have a call right now and have to go. So I've told you all what we expect out of you, and if these rules are broken, we will pursue another avenue. I might bring Mother over to watch you guys. She's very bored since Dad died. If you think I'm strict, wait 'til you live with Grandma for a few days."

As Zack headed for the exit, Kim said, "I'll meet you outside."

He nodded okay.

———⟫●⟪———

Kim wanted a few minutes with Kathy. The guys had left the room by now. Kathy got up to leave.

Kim asked, "Can we talk?"

"I'm listening," Kathy said with disdain.

As a former teacher, Kim had dealt with numerous girls with attitudes as they went through their adolescent years. So this was familiar terrain for her. "You know, we are the only women in the house—"

"I know that." Kathy retorted.

Her behavior disappointed Kim. She thought, since she was dating her father, she might be a little more gracious. Since she felt she wasn't getting anywhere with the conversation. Kim said sternly, "Just remember what your father and I said earlier, little lady."

They locked eyes for a few seconds until Kathy turned away. Kim made her way to the door.

"I don't like you, heffa," Kathy said under her breath but loud enough for Kim to hear it.

Just before she opened the door, Kim turned around. "I heard that comment."

Before Zack left the next morning, Kim told him how Kathy had disrespected her, so another meeting with his kids was in order. Again, they met downstairs in the game room.

"I decided that we need to talk. So you go first, Kathy."

She glowered at her father. He stared back. Kathy rolled her eyes and folded her arms across her ample breasts.

God, what happened to my little girl?

"I'll start, Dad," Johnny said.

"Okay, Son."

Johnny stammered "I ... I ... well ... we." He glanced over at Kathy and then back at his father.

Presently, they were sitting on the couch, and Zack was seated in a folding chair, facing them.

"We feel you abandoned us."

Zack felt a twinge of guilt. "How so?"

"When you got married to your last wife."

Zack jumped in again. "Diane?"

"Yeah, I believe that was her name." Johnny said sarcastically. "And you guys had a son."

Zack wasn't sure where they were going with this. "What's your little brother have to do with this?"

Then Kathy angrily spouted. "Half, he's our half-brother."

"Okay, okay, missy. He's still your brother." Zack snapped.

Kathy continued. "And when he was born, you didn't have the same love for us like you used to."

Zack's head was spinning now. "That's not true. Things changed, but not my love." He scratched his bald head in frustration. "I'm sorry if you guys feel that way. Just because I had a new wife and a new kid didn't mean I loved you any less."

"Sure, that's why you cast us aside like we never existed." Kathy unfolded her arms and pointed her finger at her father.

"Suga, I'm so sorry you feel that way. I came to visit as much as I could. I had to work, and with the new baby—"

"All I'm hearing," Kathy replied with more anger in her voice, "is excuses, excuses."

Zack shot upright, knocking the chair over. "Watch your mouth, young lady. You will respect Kim and me in this household. I don't know what kind of home Jinette used to run, but I will not tolerate you all getting smart with the grown-ups in this house. Do I make myself clear?"

They both tucked their heads, and with eyes downcast, they mumbled, "Yes, sir."

"This meeting is over."

If they wouldn't listen to him, Kim didn't have a prayer. He'd have to call his mother.

Chapter 13

Nasty felt excited about hiring Maria. He thought she was sexy and pretty. Most of the women who worked at his strip clubs and escort business had gone with him in order to get their jobs.

Maria will be my next conquest, he thought.

But he would take his time getting her in bed. Right now, she would be a great asset to his collection, especially with her exotic looks. Needless to say, the other strippers didn't take too kindly to her being there. They turned up their noses at her in the dressing room.

Bambi, a shapely, thirty-something with bright red hair, said aloud, "Who is that? Who that bitch think she is coming up in here?"

Since his office was in the back of to the dressing room, Nasty heard everything they were saying, so he got up from his chair, opened the dressing room door, and stepped in.

He cleared his throat. "If anyone … I repeat … if any one of you has a problem with my new hire, hit the damn door! Right now! I run this operation. Do I make myself clear?"

Bambi bowed her head and shut her mouth.

Nasty turned toward Maria, who was sitting on a stool in front of a row of lights. "Her name is Maria. She's very pretty, as y'all can see that. And sweet as far as I can tell." He chuckled.

Maria looked up at him smugly.

"Get up, sweetie," Nasty said.

She slowly stood up. She was wearing a red teddy that hugged her body like a glove.

"Turn around."

She obliged.

"With an ass and face like this, I just couldn't turn her down."

Maria's cheeks reddened, and she sat back on her stool.

"So you gals make her feel at home. Introduce yourselves."

———⟫●⟪———

For the next five minutes, the thinly clad ladies in high heels strolled over, said their names, and shook her hand. Caitlyn felt a few might have been genuine, but that most were not; the girls did it only because Nasty told them to. So after the forced greet-and-meet thing was over, Nasty asked Maria to follow him to his office.

Clutching her small purse, she sat on a small sofa in front of his desk.

"Maria, I know absolutely nothing about you."

She shrugged her shoulders.

"So are you from here? You know, Virginia."

"No, I'm from New Orleans," she lied.

"Okay, okay, I get it. You Creole. How'd you end up in Tilton, Virginia?"

She sighed. "Long story."

"So you don't want to discuss it," Nasty said.

"No, I don't," Maria replied.

He reached into his pocket, got a small key, and unlocked the desk drawer. He rifled through a stack of bills. "Here's $800 so you can buy yourself some more outfits. Or do whatever you have to do with the money. I rarely do this, but I think you're going to be somebody special."

"Are you sure?" She stared at the money now resting on the desk.

"Absolutely. Trust me. I'll get it back. I just feel you will make a lot of money for me."

She thanked him and picked up the money.

"Can I get a hug?" Nasty asked.

Nasty stepped from around his desk. They embraced. Something twinged in the back of her mind, but it refused to surface.

Before Caitlyn left, she asked, "How much do you get from my dancing?"

"Ten percent from you. And that's pretty good considering I charge the other girls fifteen percent. That's between us. Those other bitches don't need to know my business."

Chapter 14

Kim stepped inside her house and tossed the keys on the counter. *What a long night.* To top it off, she had to drive Zack to the airport at five. She looked forward to a hot bath and a warm bed. A yawn escaped. *Scratch the bath. The bed is calling.* She crossed the living room, dodged a model plane Johnny had no doubt left out, and then felt something squish beneath her shoe. *Oh God, not now.*

All she wanted to do was go to bed. She briefly thought about not looking. *That's it. I could pretend it never happened.* But the smell drifted up and assaulted her nose. There was no pretending. She lifted her foot and stared down at the fresh poop that Fluffy had left behind.

"Kathy, did you let Fluffy out?"

There was no reply.

Kim stormed over to Kathy's room. She could hear a voice yammering away on the other side. Kim threw open the door. "Didn't you hear me?"

Kathy let out an exaggerated sigh. "Brenda, just a sec." She pulled the phone away from her ear. "Don't you knock?"

"Don't answer my question with a question. When I call you, you answer."

"I was on the phone," Kathy replied.

"I thought your father took away your phone privileges."

"So," Kathy said. "He ain't here."

Kim felt her blood boil. "Hang up the phone, and clean up the dog shit in the living room."

"I ain't cleaning up no dog shit. Let Johnny do it."

Kim took a deep breath. *Count to ten.* She got as far as three.

"Fluffy is your responsibility."

"So," Kathy said.

"So, clean up his crap."

"Uh-uh. I ain't cleaning up no dog shit," Kathy said.

Kim tightened her hands. She wanted to strangle that girl. It would be so easy.

"Maybe you should call one of your little meetings about that." Kathy then turned her back on Kim and raised the phone to her ear. "That was just dad's stupid GF going all queen bitch on me."

That was it. Kim stormed across the room and snatched the phone from Kathy's grip.

"Hey," Kathy said. "What the hell?"

"You have lost your phone privileges. You can have this back when your time is up." Kim shoved the phone into her pocket. "Now, go to the living room and clean up the poop."

Kathy stormed out. Kim turned to go when she spotted an open box turned on its side and tucked under the bed. A brand-new Prada handbag spilled out from the box. *Where did Kathy get the money for that?* She didn't have a job, and Zack was a cop, so there was no way her allowance would cover it. *Leave it alone, Kim.* But she couldn't. She was a cop, too.

Zack's mother, Mrs. Jane Townes, was eighty years old. She still had most of faculties. Since the death of her beloved husband, she felt lonely. Slightly bent over and with a thick head of white wavy hair, Granny was still feisty. In her younger days, she was a strict disciplinarian. And Zack and the rest of his siblings could vouch for that.

Kim went to pick her up. She always called her Mrs. Jane. When she arrived, they hugged, and Kim helped her to pack enough of her stuff for a month. And that depended on how things with her grandkids went. If they acted okay and didn't show off, she'd stay longer. If not, she'd just head back to her place.

When they pulled into the driveway, the kids greeted her warmly, giving her kisses and hugs. Next, they helped her with her luggage. Once everybody was settled in, Kim began to prepare supper. Granny took a seat at the kitchen table.

Adjacent to the kitchen was the living room where the boys played video games on a flat-screen television. And sitting over in a far corner of the living room, Kathy was completely into a conversation she was having on her cell phone. All the while, Granny was taking it all in.

"Kids nowadays," she said, "are too preoccupied with all these electronic and digital gadgets."

"Amen to that." Kim placed a chicken in the oven. On the top aisles were steamed broccoli and corn on the cob. "You are spot-on, Mrs. Jane."

Kim took a break from cooking, sat down, and chatted with Mrs. Jane for nearly an hour, just the right amount of time for everything to be done.

After Kim prepared Mrs. Jane's plate, she hollered. "Supper is ready, you guys. But wash your hands first."

The boys instantly dropped the video station controls, jumped up, and raced to the bathroom. Kathy had heard what Kim had said, but she kept talking on her cell phone. Kim regretted giving Kathy back her phone privileges. It had brought some peace, but the cost might have been too high. Still, she needed to reach the girl.

"Supper is ready," Kim said again.

Kathy gave a dismissive wave, rolled her eyes, turned her head, and kept talking.

Mrs. Jane watched the whole episode. "If she did that to me, I'd take her cell phone from her. Obviously, little missy has a problem with taking orders. If I were younger, I would have went upside her head before I knew it. I didn't take no mess back then. Ask Zack and the rest of my kids. Just like the Bible says. Spare the rod; spoil the child."

Kim was pretty sure a beat down wasn't going to get Kathy talking. Also, it was mostly illegal these days. So, she said nothing.

Chapter 15

At two in the afternoon, Zack's plane touched down at the El Paso airport. Waves of heat were rising from the asphalt. As he picked up his luggage, a deputy from the El Paso PD approached him and introduced himself. They shook hands and headed out to the patrol car in the parking lot. A wall of hot, dry heat engulfed them.

Beads of sweat instantly appeared on Zack's baldhead. "Damn, it's hot out here."

The young, chubby deputy answered with a chuckle. "Welcome to El Paso. The weatherman said it would be a hundred and seven today. And with the heat index, it should feel like a hundred and twelve."

Zack groaned. Maybe coming to El Paso wasn't such a good idea after all. They got in the car and made small talk on the way to the station. Thankfully, the AC worked, and the chubby deputy blasted it full bore. And when they got there, Chief Sanders gave Zack a hearty handshake.

Standing nearly Zack's height, the very tan, fifty-something chief resembled Robert Redford in his younger years, with his sandy blond hair and moustache. Chief Sanders briefed him on the drug war and trade that was spilling across the border from Juarez, a stone's throw from El Paso.

"Ever hear of the Zetas?" Chief Sanders asked.

"Can't say that I have," Zack replied.

"They're a Mexican cartel that operate out of Juarez."

Zack nodded.

The chief continued. "Their calling card is decapitations."

Zack perked up. "That sounds like our boys."

The chief nodded. "Real nasty bunch. They're good at what they do."

"And what's that?" Zack asked.

"Hired guns and some drug trafficking."

"Hired guns?" Zack asked. "They ex-military?"

The chief shook his head. He pulled out a rag and dabbed it in his glass of water. He wrung it out over the back of his neck before continuing. "Nah, but they're well trained. Rumor has it the DEA created them to take down the Narcos."

"Serious?"

"Dead, and that ain't the worst of it."

"I'm almost afraid to ask," Zack said.

"Damn feds equipped them, too."

"So, we're talking some firepower."

"Yep. Once Calderon declared war on the cartels, all hell broke loose. Damn border's been like a DMZ ever since."

"Calderon?"

"Felipe Calderon. El Presidente, at least he was back in oh-six."

"And the Zetas?"

The chief stood up and paced a bit. He stopped in front of a map showing the border. "They worked with Calderon for a time. Once enough cartels fell, a vacuum opened up. They switched sides and filled it."

Zack frowned. "And now they're all the way up in Virginia."

All the way up in my backyard.

"Sounds like it, friend."

Zack chewed this over for a bit. It sounded plausible, but he had to know for sure. "Can I get a look at them?"

The chief sat back down, picked up his glass of water, and gulped it down. "That would require a trip to Juarez."

"Is that a problem?"

"Not if you don't mind getting shot at."

Zack did mind, but he also needed to know. "When can we go?"

The next day, Chief Sanders thought it would be a good idea for Zack and other agents from ICE, ATF, DEA, and Border Patrol to walk across the bridge over to Juarez to see drug trade firsthand. So everyone was dressed in body armor and riot gear and armed with a Sig 9mm and AR-15. They were immediately struck by the abject poverty. Seeing it from across the border was one thing, but up close was completely different. Shacks covered the dusty hillside. They were literally made of things one would find in a landfill: wooden pallets, faded tarps, and plastic, rusty pieces of tin. And everything seemed to be held together with wire, nails, or rope. Mingled among the makeshift shacks were fortified mansions or Narco houses.

Chapter 16

Jose DeJesus was as ruthless as he was handsome. His copper-toned skin glowed in the sunlight on his six-foot athletic frame, accentuated by the closely cropped, tousled hair. Born twenty-five years ago in Juarez, Mexico, he felt the sting of poverty at a young age. His father abandoned him and his mother when he was a toddler. They had to eke out a life as best they could. His mother worked odd low-paying jobs just to put food on the table. And when she wasn't able to do that, she taught him how to beg on the street, especially from tourists who came from the states just across the border; they always gave more money than the locals. Some tourists could be mean, throwing money on the ground just to see him scramble to pick it up.

Jose vowed to himself that he would never be the victim of poverty, and he would get out of this rut by any means necessary when he was old enough. As he grew older, he would see older boys riding around town in fancy, tricked-out, expensive vehicles with shiny rims and wearing the latest shoes and clothes. So one day, he was so intrigued about how they were able to have such nice things that he stopped a teenage boy who had pulled up to the curb, jumped out, and run inside a bodega. Jose asked him what he did to live a glamorous life with the flashy clothes and vehicles. The young boy told him he belonged to the Zeta gang, and he had to put in some work in order to join.

"Put in work." Jose frowned as the gangbanger hurried past him. "What's that?"

"Meet me here tomorrow." The gangbanger glanced down at his Rolex. "The same time."

Jose was giddy. Tomorrow couldn't come soon enough.

They met the next morning. The gangbanger explained that, in order to join the Zeta gang and drug cartel, putting in work meant stealing from and sometimes beating up members from the Sinola cartel, their archrivals.

In short order, Jose rose through the ranks. With his first Sinola beating, he nearly killed the guy. Next, he would graduate to decapitations, their calling card. It wasn't an issue for him because violence was part of his DNA now. Besides, if violence were part of the so-called good life to keep him from being poor, count him in.

But as the killings escalated in Juarez, he felt the heat, so he snuck across the border into El Paso, Texas, as an illegal. And once he was over in the States, through his contacts, he was able to get a birth certificate stating he was born in the United States. And when that was finished, his drug operation was off and running in no time. A few years later, law enforcement was onto him in El Paso.

He lay low for a few months and lowered his profile, pretending to be a migrant worker. But the cops there didn't let up. So a couple migrants told him the Pruitt farm in Virginia would be a change of scenery from all the attention he was getting from the cops.

Jose made his move to Virginia as a migrant at the Pruitt tobacco farm. The owner, Sammy Pruitt, was incredulous about him being a migrant, especially after he pulled up to his house in a black, tricked-out Escalade, but he hired him anyway.

After settling in his new surroundings, Jose moved his main drug operation to Virginia. While in the drug trade, Jose had met people of many stripes, so it wasn't any surprise when he met the mayor of Tilton, Ray Brownlow, who happened to be an addict. But that wasn't his problem. Jose felt having him as a friend or moreover an ally would be advantageous for pushing his drugs.

DeJesus stood on top of his Narco house nestled along a hillside. He was peering through a pair of binoculars. Flanking DeJesus sides were his friends. Through his main contact, Mayor Brownlow, DeJesus found out some stinking cop, a bald *punta* named Zack Townes, was coming to El Paso, but he never thought the pig would have the nerve to come over into Juarez. El Paso was one thing, but Juarez? That was disrespect.

"I can't believe that asshole cop and his minions are in my country. Snooping around like his badge means something," DeJesus said more to himself than to his friends. Anger was rising up in him every second. "The big, bald-headed cop don't fucking know we are Zetas. We take no prisoners." DeJesus slammed down the binoculars against the cement wall on the roof, cracking them. DeJesus continued his rant as he thumbed his chest with his fist. "It's time we showed him I'm the law here." He shook his AK-47. "And this is my badge."

Chapter 17

"Let me guess," Zack said sarcastically, peering at the expensive houses as they entered the police station. "The mansions are the best homes that drug money can buy."

"Si," Jose Contreas, the chief of police in Juarez, said.

They had just strolled into the relatively small police station. And the pudgy, middle-aged chief greeted them warmly.

"Thank you guys for coming."

"I gather you have your hands full down here," said a skinny DEA agent.

"That's putting it mildly," he said with a heavy Mexican accent. "This place, Juarez, is the last stop before getting into America. It's the gateway. We get more traffic of people trying to get into the States than does Tijuana just across from California. Also, we definitely get more violence and murders, too. Thousands and thousands of immigrants are coming from all over Central and South America, desperately trying to get into the States. And the coyotes, the ones who pay for their entry into America, let them down, not to mention the drug lords.

"How so?" Zack asked.

"Well, the coyotes take their money sometimes even before they make it to the border, and the drug dealers would take them hostage in order to get ransom money from a relative or friend in the United States. And if they don't pay, they are killed a lot of times. It's just a big mess."

———⇒●⇐———

The black van eased down the dusty street in front of the police station. DeJesus was wielding his AK-47 as he stood bent over inside the van with his neck touching the top of the van. Then the driver sped right in front of the police station and stopped.

DeJesus suddenly slid the door open, popped out, and bellowed, "Die you fucking assholes!"

Much like his favorite actor, Al Pacino, did in Scarface, he sprayed bullets inside the station in a side-to-side motion.

———⇒●⇐———

Shards of glass rained down, and the riddled curtains jumped up and down. Everybody hit the floor and took cover. And when DeJesus's clip was empty, he hopped back inside the van. And the driver stomped the gas pedal, and the van tires squealed as it fishtailed down the street. Once everyone inside realized what had happened, they returned fire, but it was too late. The van was gone.

The atmosphere was very tense in the station. Zack and the other agents nervously stood upright, brushing shattered glass off their clothes.

"Help! Help me! I've been hit," said the female customs agent who had befriended Zack earlier. Zack rushed over to assist her. She was leaning against the wall, holding her bleeding right arm. "It hurts so bad." She grimaced through clenched teeth.

Zack stared at her wound. It was bleeding profusely. The bullet had entered her right arm just above her elbow. Zack leaned in closer and could see torn flesh and bone fragments mingled among the blood constantly spewing from the gaping gash.

"It looks like the bullet hit an artery or vein," Zack said. "I need to make a tourniquet. Somebody get me a pipe or stick, something I can twist around her arm. Throw that curtain over here."

Chief Contreas gave Zack his police stick that was in his drawer. Then Zack tore strips of curtains and made a tourniquet. The bleeding was stopped. Every few minutes, Zack would release the pressure from the tourniquet.

Chief Contreas said shakily, "See what I mean."

"How often does this happen?" asked a female ATF agent.

"Maybe once a month. But the other times, the shootings occurred at night. This is the first time it has happened during the daytime."

Over the next ten minutes, the American contingent hastily made its way back across the border. The shooting was too much for comfort. But before leaving, they thanked the chief and shook his hand, and they were out the door.

Chapter 18

K im got the call. A street sweeper had found a middle-aged, naked, male Caucasian dead in a parked Jag. This was the first killing she had been to without Zack. It felt a little strange. At the crime scene, several civilians had gathered around the car.

"I need for everybody to stand back." Kim extended her hands. "You all might be contaminating my crime scene."

They obeyed.

"Where's the grounds guy?" Kim looked around the crowd.

An old African-American man threw up his hand.

She waved him over. "So my dispatcher said you were the first to find the abandoned car with the body in it."

"Yes. That's true."

Kim broke out her pen and pad. The forensics van and Ken Banks, the medical examiner investigator, both pulled up at the same time. It was like both were attached at the hip. First thing the forensics team did was cordon off the Jag with yellow police tape.

Kim then asked, "So what happened?

"Well …" He sighed. "As I made my way to the garage, I noticed it right off the bat."

"What?"

"The car in the parking lot. I thought that was unusual. And as I was filling up the street sweeper, I wondered why someone would leave a nice car like that in this parking lot."

"Why do you say that?" Kim kept writing.

"A lot of kids in the neighboring area are known for breaking into cars, especially expensive ones like this one."

"All right. Keep going."

"I thought I best go over there and see if something were wrong. And lo and behold, that's when I saw that body in the backseat."

"Did you notice anything else?"

He scratched his scruffy white hair. "Naw, that's about it. That's when I got back on the ride and told my boss. And he called y'all."

"Okay, okay. Thank you, sir."

Ken Banks had just wrapped up his part and nodded for the CSI team to jump in and do their thing. Kim had seen a bullet hole in the chest and wondered what Ken's take was on what happened to the vic.

She playfully said, "So, Mr. Medical Examiner Investigator, Ken Banks, what do you think happened?"

"Well, it wasn't a suicide. That's for sure."

"Why do you say that?"

"There's no stippling on his hands from a self-inflected wound. But there is some stippling around the hole in the chest area."

"So someone shot him at close range. And without his shirt on."

"Correct."

"Sounds like someone was pretty upset."

"You can say that again." Ken added. "I don't do ballistics, but it's obvious it was a small caliber weapon. And he had bruises on his lower legs and thighs. Under his body was a pair of soiled pink panties." Ken shrugged. "I assume a female wore them, but who knows these days?"

"Perhaps a sexual encounter gone terribly wrong?"

"That's your job, not mine."

"What about time of death? Now that's your turf."

"He's not at full rigor, so I'd say six to eight hours. But Dr. Powell will narrow it down even further with the other markers she uses."

Chapter 19

K im picked up Zack from Raleigh-Durham at nine in the morning. He had arrived ten minutes earlier, and he was retrieving his luggage. She parked out front, and when he saw her, his eyes lit up, and he smiled. She quickly got out of the car. They embraced and kissed.

"I missed you, hon," Kim said.

"Likewise, sweetie," Zack replied.

She popped the trunk. Zack put in his luggage and then closed the trunk.

As they climbed in the car, Kim asked, "How was Texas?"

"Hot," Zack replied.

"Just hot?"

"And dusty."

"Just hot and dusty?"

"Yup."

"Anything more to add?"

"Nope," Zack said. "That just about sums it up."

Kim took the off ramp onto I-40. Traffic wasn't too bad at that time in the morning.

"So, did you find out anything that could help us with the Tuck killing?"

"Yeah, I think so." Zack paused for a spell. Then he laughed.

"What's so funny?" Kim glanced over at him.

"Before I continue with the Tuck case, I have to tell you. I almost got killed."

"And that's funny?"

"No, this is not a joke." His expression had changed. His voice was serious now. "Me and some other agents, you know, the alphabet guys—DEA, ICE, and ATF—along with the border patrol and custom officers, crossed the border into Mexico to get briefed by Jurarez's chief about the drug business. And before we knew it, while in his office no less, a hail of bullets was shattering glass, and we all hit the damn floor. Even the chief was on his belly."

"That's very dangerous."

"Tell me about it. No shit," Zack said with a small smile. "But anyway, it's a miracle nobody was killed. However, an agent was hit, but it wasn't life-threatening, and we returned fire."

"Damn. So were you able to get some information?"

"Yeah, I think, or it's just a hunch right now. But the Zeta cartel could have killed Mr. Tuck. Their MO or calling card is killing by beheading. I wonder if those young Mexicans on the Pruitt farm may have been involved with his murder."

"That BOLO is still out on their black SUV," Kim said. "The department has stopped several vehicles like theirs but with no Texas tags. Of course, they could have switched them out and put on Virginia tags as far as we know."

Zack sighed. "Yeah, that's a possibility. So how are things going at the house?"

Kim hesitated and took a deep breath. "I went and got your mother."

"Okay."

"How are she and the kids doing? Are they getting along?"

"For the most part."

He looked at Kim sideways as his voice dropped. "What happened with the kids and Mother?"

"Nothing."

"Let me have it. I bet it's Kathy."

"Yep."

"Okay," Zack said slowly.

Kim told him what happened. She wanted to say something about the bag, but she wasn't sure how to broach the subject. Zack must have taken her hesitation to mean she was finished telling him about Kathy.

"Changing gears," he said. "What's the latest at the station?"

"There was another killing."

"I'll be damned," Zack said. "I leave town for several days, and everything goes to hell."

Kim glanced over at him and shrugged her shoulders. "Hey, I'm not the one that got shot at."

He let out a breath. "Was the vic male, female, black, or white?"

Kim's cell phone rang. It was in the middle console.

"Get that for me, hon."

Zack picked up the phone and looked at the screen. "It's the forensic lab."

Kim said, "Maybe they got something on the new murder."

Zack put it on the speaker. "Townes."

A young male on the other end excitedly asked, "You're back, Detective?"

Zack thought about being a wiseass and saying, "Hell naw, I'm still in Texas," but declined.

"What's up?"

"We got some good trace evidence from the latest vic, the white male found shot in the Jag." He paused. "Before I continue, did Sarge tell you about him?"

"No, she was ready to when you called."

"Okay, okay. The vic is a white, middle-aged male found shot by a small caliber weapon. Ballistics is on that part of the case right at this moment. I just talked to them before I called Sarge. Any way, we got great DNA samples from a pair of stained pink panties, chewing gum, cigarette butts, and strands of female hair, all from the same source."

"Good. Were you able to come up with a name?"

"Absolutely. Skylar Hicks. She has priors. Grand larceny, trespassing, bad checks, brandishing a weapon, and assault and battery."

"Damn, she sounds like a career criminal."

"I'll say." The young man laughed. "She's on probation. It says right here that she works as a stripper at a place called Naughty Women."

"You have a residence listed?"

"Oaks on Forty-Ninth."

Chapter 20

Soon after Zack hung up, the dispatcher said with panic in her voice, "There's another dead body on the other side of town, Detective. You guys are a few miles away."

"We're on it," Zack said.

After getting the address, Kim pushed down on the gas and turned on her blue light as she raced down the street. They pulled up outside the garage. They grabbed their .40 calibers and cautiously made their way for the front entrance.

Slightly crouched in his police stance with his sidearm out in front of him and his partner likewise a few feet behind him, Zack slowly pushed open the cracked front door. He stepped inside the stuffy living room. His gaze gave the place a cursory look as he swept his gun wherever his eyes went. Still in a steady sweeping motion, he entered deeper into the residence.

"Anybody home!" Zack screamed as the unmistakable odor of Clorox attacked his nose as he entered the living room and headed down the hallway. Then Zack quipped, "Smells like someone was trying to clean something."

Kim went in the opposite direction as she went toward the bedrooms in the back of the house, making sure nobody else was there, especially a potential killer.

As Zack inched his way down the hall, he saw red specks on the polished hardwood floor of what he took to be blood. Right before he came to the end of the hall, he saw an upturned coffee table and a body resting supine. It was a naked white male, fortyish, with his eyes and mouth opened. And as his eyes traveled to the lower body, he saw he was minus his penis.

"Hell," he said to himself. "Don't see that too often."

A few feet from the vic was his manhood, shriveled up like a white prune.

"Oh my God." Zack let out a little breath.

Kim sidled next to him. "Everything's clear."

Blood splatter was all over the couch and hardwood floor.

Kim squinted down at the body. "Seems like he got a double whammy. He got his pecker cut off and his throat slit. Look at that gash about his Adam's apple."

"Damn, somebody must have been mad as hell with him." Zack added.

Ken Banks arrived. "I see we meet again, Sergeant Patterson. So, how long has it been since the last murder?"

"Around twenty-four hours," Kim replied.

Then Ken nodded at Zack. "Glad to see you are back in town, Detective."

Zack chuckled. "I don't know if I'm glad to be back or not with these killings going on. We'll let you do your thing, Ken. If you need anything, we will be outside."

As they exited the house, the forensics team pulled up in a white van. The two techs were dressed in all white. They were a male and female in their twenties. They jumped out the van, hustled to the back, opened the door, donned their footies, grabbed their gear, and headed inside the house.

Zack and Kim went to the cruiser, got out a roll of yellow police tape, and cordoned off the front of the house. Next, they took a seat on the hood of the cruiser and waited.

"What was the name of that woman that cut off her husband's penis?" Zack asked Kim.

"You know it was several years back."

"Wasn't her last name Burnett? A Lisa Burnett?" Kim tried to come up with her name.

"No, no." Zack scratched his bald head. "I believe her last name did start with a B, though. But it's not Burnett."

Kim said, "It escapes me right now, Zack."

"Well, we probably got a serial killer on our hands. And he or she has lost his or her damn mind. What is this? The third killing in two weeks: Tuck, the dead guy in the Jag, and now this dude."

As Zack was speaking, the vic was wheeled out on a gurney. His body was stuffed in a black body bag with "Coroner" and "Medical Examiner" stenciled on the sides.

Ken Banks ambled toward Zack. He still had on his latex gloves and gave Zack the vic's driver's license. "I think you might need this. I found it under the couch."

Zack asked him to lay it on the hood of the cruiser. He didn't want to touch it or contaminate it. "Kyle Cohen, white male, forty-five."

Before Ken could turn on his heel to leave, Zack stopped him. "Hey, Ken, what was the name of that woman—"

Ken cut him off. "Lorena Bobbitt."

"Damn, that's it, Kim."

"I figured you guys would ask that. The techs and I were trying to come up with her name. And her husband was named John Bobbitt. It happened back in the nineties."

"Yep," Zack said. "You are so right."

Before Zack and Kim left Mr. Cohen's residence, they wanted to go over a few things.

"Let's see if there was a forced entry," Zack said. "Go around back, Kim, and check the windows and doors."

"Okay," Kim said. "I'll check them out."

When Zack stepped back inside the house, the forensics team was wrapping up their job. Each tech had several paper bags of evidence as all saw the detective come into the kitchen area.

"How did things go?" Zack inquired.

"We collected a lot," the female tech said. "From trace evidence and latent prints from inside the red Corvette in the garage to bloody footprints in the bathroom and skin on the upturned coffee table."

"Sounds promising," Zack said. "So it's all right for us to move about now."

"Sure," the male tech said. "We got everything we need."

By now, Kim was in the house, following Zack into the living room. "There was no forced entry as far as the windows and door in the back."

Zack stopped when he got to the living room and rubbed his chin as he stared at the bloody section where the body was. "So, what do you think happened, Kim?"

"Since there wasn't any forced entry, Mr. Cohen knew his attacker. It's probably a female. Maybe a girlfriend or wife that got mad at him for cheating and whacked off his pecker."

Zack waited a bit before responding. "Could be, or perhaps he got lucky at a club. Or maybe he picked up a prostitute, and they came back to his home."

"I wouldn't exactly call that lucky," Kim said.

Zack thought of the shriveled penis. "No, I guess not."

Chapter 21

At nine the next morning, Zack and Kim made it to Skylar Hicks's apartment. Zack rapped on the door. There was nothing. He knocked on it a little harder.

There was some movement inside. Finally, a tall blonde cracked the door as far as the night latch would allow. Her sleepy blue eyes bulged when she realized it was the cops.

"Detective Townes." Zack flashed his badge. "Are you Skylar Hicks?"

"Yes, yes." She stammered.

"Could we come in? We have a few questions we would like to ask you."

"Okay," she said nervously as she closed the door, unlatched it, and opened it again. "Come on in."

Kim glanced around the living room and thought it was nice but too glittery or loud for her taste.

Skylar was in her nightgown. "Have a seat while I get my robe."

They sat on a comfortable lilac cotton sofa. Next to it was a white end table that held a lamp that lit up the room. When she reentered the living room, she was holding a pack of Salems and a lighter, the same type of cigarette that was found in the car.

She shook one out of the pack, shakily brought it to her lips, and lit it. "What's … what's going on?" She stuttered.

"Where were you last Friday?" Zack asked.

"At work."

Kim jumped in. "You are a stripper, right?"

"That's correct."

"What else happened that night?" Zack asked.

Skylar thought about the question hard and pulled on her Salem. "Nothing comes to mind at the moment. Just my regular routine."

"Did you have customers you'd see or have relations with outside your job?"

"Yes, I'd say I had clients outside of my work."

"Did you know Mr. Stewart?

"No. His name doesn't ring a bell."

"Okay." Zack reached into his front shirt pocket and pulled out a photo of the deceased man. "Maybe this picture will ring that bell."

She put her cigarette in an ashtray on the end table. She grabbed the photo with both hands and studied it for a long spell. Tears began to roll down her cheeks. "What happened to him?"

"That's why we are here," Kim answered.

Skylar sighed.

"So, in order to make your case or clear your name, we have to know what happened that night."

Nervously grabbing her cigarette from the ashtray and taking a long drag as if gaining strength from it, she exhaled the smoke. "Well, in order for me to get to the night in question y'all are asking about, I need to give some background on our relationship."

They nodded.

"Okay. Yeah, I recall him. He was flashy. We call them types 'high rollers' at the club, Mr. Big Time or Mr. Vegas. He was no exception. He wore expensive clothes and drove expensive foreign cars. Like that Jag. But he would sit by himself and buy expensive drinks of course."

"Can you speed it up a little? You know, get to the facts," Zack said.

"All right. All right. So one night, Mr. Stewart tucked a hundred-dollar bill in my G-string. And I was amazed. So the next thing you know, we started dating. We dated, I guess, maybe six months. I later found out he was married. But he said he and his wife had an understanding, whatever that meant. And then the arguments started."

"About what? His wife?" Kim asked.

Ms. Hicks gave a little laugh. "No, it wasn't his wife. It was about silly shit. I guess I was getting jealous because he was showing other girls more attention."

"What about the money?" Zack asked.

"Of course, I thought the money he was spending on them was mine. But not to a point of killing him."

"Is that right?" Kim said.

"Yeah, that's right. I'm not that damn crazy. I know you guys know I'm on probation."

"Absolutely," Zack said.

"So, what happened again that Friday night?" Kim asked.

"I told myself that I'd have sex with him one last time. I know what y'all are thinking. Yes, it was for the money. Hell, I got bills to pay. So we got together and had sex. That's it."

"Why was he shot?" Kim asked.

"I dunno. I didn't do it."

"You have an extensive rap sheet," Zack said.

"Hell, I know that. We just talked about my probation a second ago. I paid my debt to society."

"Your DNA is in his vehicle and on his body."

"Well, we were together. I'd think so. I promise you I didn't murder anybody." She wrung her hands in frustration. There was a short pause. "What did I leave in his vehicle?"

"Pink panties with your DNA in them. And not to mention the chewing gum, your hair, and the same cigarettes you've been smoking this morning," Zack said.

"I rode with him to his place. I told you that. Don't mean I killed him. You have the gun?"

"We haven't found it yet," Zack said. "Do you have it?'

"Hell naw!" she screamed. "This ain't no damn game."

Zack and Kim stood upright.

Zack said, "Skylar, do you mind going with us to the station for further questioning?"

"I'll go with y'all, but I didn't do it!" She began to cry again. "Y'all need to be checking out the other girls, like Maria. Hell, she dated him longer than I did. She probably killed him."

"You can get dressed first," Zack said.

She got up and went to put on a pair of jeans and T-shirt.

When she was completely dressed, they all left the building. Skylar flopped down in the backseat of the car, just sniffled, and tucked her head as Zack pulled out of the apartment's parking lot.

Chapter 22

Nasty asked Maria if she wanted to ride with him on a business trip into the mountains next to West Virginia so they could get to know each other better. She said she would love to go with him. Nasty had chosen a five-star Marriott that overlooked the Appalachian mountain range. He thought it would be an ideal place for a special occasion such as theirs, but more to the point, he could hardly contain the lust that was popping out of his pores and badly wanted to get into Maria's pants. And having his little so-called meeting there was an afterthought.

Nasty had paid for an executive suite with his Visa the day before. This was his third trip there, and he liked the amenities it provided, especially the Jacuzzi.

At eight in the evening, they arrived at the Marriott from the three-hour trip. Once they settled into their room, they both crashed on the bed and took an hour-long nap. Nasty got up first and took a shower. When he came out, he saw Maria holding a bucket of ice with a chilled bottle of Dom Perignon inside.

"I see we already have us some expensive champagne to drink, Nasty." Maria smiled.

"Absolutely, I try to plan ahead, sweetie." Then he turned and looked at the clock on the wall. "Dinner should be here at nine thirty."

"Damn," Maria said. "Let me hit the shower, too."

No sooner had Nasty kicked back in the recliner, than he heard a soft knock at the door. He got up and peeped through the peephole. It was the female concierge with a dolly that held their dinner. He quickly opened the door. She nodded at him as she pushed it toward the table in the kitchen. The concierge placed the two plates of roasted lamb, asparagus, and poached potatoes with a dish of caviar and crackers on the table. Nasty thanked her. But before she left, he gave her a fifty-dollar tip. He was starving as he stared at the food. Then suddenly, his attention was on Maria as she stepped in toward him.

"What do you think, darling?"

She was stunning, all dolled up with the hair pulled in a ponytail and wearing a white negligee and matching thong.

Nasty's eyes lit up at the sight of her. "I know dinner is served. But my God, I can't wait for my dessert, if you know what I mean."

"Yeah, I got you, darling."

It wasn't twenty minutes later after polishing off the great meal that they were in the Jacuzzi, sipping on the Dom Perignon from stem glasses. They hugged and kissed. Nasty pressed his manhood against her inner thigh.

Maria whispered, "Take it easy with me. I never had a man like this before."

Nasty laughed. "Don't worry, baby. I'll only give you as much as you can stand."

For the next hour, Nasty made passionate love to Maria. He felt good, like in his younger days. When they finished, they both were exhausted and went to sleep.

———————>•<———————

Maria slept late. It was noon the next day when laughter woke her. She slipped on a robe, went to the bedroom door, cracked it, and peeped in the living room. Two men were sitting with Nasty as they all laughed. She could make out one was white and the other was Hispanic. *So this must be the business Nasty was talking about.*

Beer bottles were on the small table between them. The Hispanic guy, or so she thought, was very handsome as they got up to take the empty bottles to the kitchen area. But when she saw the other man, a shudder came over her. Was it her tormentor, or did he have a twin brother? Could it be Ray Brownlow, the bastard that raped her repeatedly and left her for dead in the desert? The piece of shit that had left a permanent scar under her eye?

She eased the door back shut. Her mind began to race as she climbed back in the bed. Why would Nasty have anything to do with him? What type of business were they in? Did she let down her guard too soon with Nasty? Maria lay in bed. She couldn't sleep. Memories of that fateful night kept replaying in her mind.

Two hours later, Nasty opened the door.

Caitlyn faked a yawn and rubbed her eyes with the palms of her hands. "How long have I been asleep? Seems like you're ready to go."

"I am. But I'm ready when you are."

Chapter 23

Many strip clubs were in and around Tilton. Some were legal, and quite a few were not. Naughty Women was legal. A huge neon sign with a young lady clad in a string bikini greeted you out front. It was the most popular strip club within the city. If there were a grading scale for such places, Naughty Women would win, hands down. Over the years, Zack had overheard hookers down at the station about to be booked chat admirably of working there, rather than on the street corner. He had been there a few times several months back.

But it was Saturday night, and the parking lot was full. A long line snaked halfway around the building. A clean-shaven, black bouncer wearing a wifebeater tank top with muscles popping out of every pore guarded a velvet rope.

Zack and his Kim made their way to the front of the line and flashed their badges. They were walked in. People were packed in like sardines. The music was so loud that they couldn't hear themselves think. Different colored lights flickered throughout the club. Dominating the floor were three elevated catwalks. One main catwalk was about fifty feet, and two narrow ones forked off toward the tables thirty feet away. At the end of all three was a shiny silver pole running from the platform to the ceiling.

As their eyes took in the place, Zack noticed two empty stools at the bar. "Let's have a seat!" He pointed toward the stools.

Kim obliged. Zack ordered them some Cokes.

The bartender, a white man about thirty, was average-sized with a hooked nose. He manned the bar and took their orders. They turned around and watched the show as they sipped their drinks. With the loud music, talking would be virtually impossible. A slew of young, shapely women paraded down the catwalk, flaunting what the good Lord blessed them with and whatever implant they could afford to enhance their bodies.

Men in business suits, blinged-out drug dealers and pimps, and your everyday wannabe baller were slipping money in the stripper's G-string.

Kim was a little annoyed about how young the girls looked. She nudged Zack and screamed, "I bet she's not even eighteen!"

"Might not be."

Nearly every stripper had one or multiple tattoos on her body. A few almost had their complete bodies covered.

Zack asked Kim, "What's with the tats?"

"I don't know. Maybe it's the in thing now."

He shrugged. "I don't get it. Perhaps it's generational."

"Yeah. That's probably what it is."

Zack spotted a waitress almost as nude as the strippers, clearing a table. "I'll be right back." He made his way through the throng. "Can I ask you a question?"

The young, petite brunette with a ring in her nose looked up at him a moment and gave him the cold shoulder as she continued doing her job. Zack showed his badge.

Her attitude changed a little. She sighed. "Yeah, what?"

"You ever see a middle-aged, slightly overweight, white male with thinning hair frequent the club?"

She let out a big laugh. "Hell, that's about half of the people that come here."

"I guess that was a bit vague." Zack continued. "I heard he came here a lot."

"Still, a bunch of the same guys come here all the time. You probably need to talk to some of the other strippers. They would probably let you know who their regular customers are and the big tippers as well."

"Can you give me a couple names of the strippers?"

"Cartier, Movado, Lexus, Mayback, and Escalade."

"Okay, thank you."

When Zack rattled off the names to Kim, she chuckled. "They sound like a line of expensive cars and watches. Young folks today. I guess, if they can't afford these high price things, why not name yourself after them?"

"Damn," he said. "I just saw a stripper a few minutes ago get a pile of money thrown on top of her."

"I think they call that making it rain."

"Raining money."

"You got it."

"Maybe she was one of those cars or watches you said earlier?"

"Could be. Let's see if we can have a chat with her. But first let's try to find the manager."

Zack asked the bartender where the manager was. He pointed to a room in the back. The detective banged on the metal door times. There was no response. He checked the doorknob. It was locked. A minute later, it crept open, and one of the strippers was naked, slightly embarrassed as she reached for her clothes and ran out of the room.

The owner, Nasty, a potbellied, bald-headed man in his fifties, was scrambling to pull up his pants over his boxers as his hefty gut jiggled.

"I guess we caught you at the wrong time." Zack smirked.

"Yeah." Nasty caught his breath. "My bartender just told me you cops were coming back here."

Kim sarcastically added. "Is that how the girls got their jobs?"

The comment caught him off guard as he slipped on a shirt. "Perhaps. Perks of being the owner and manager."

Kim kept up the pressure. "I'd bet a lot of your strippers are underage."

Getting a bit frustrated, Nasty barked. "Are you guys here to shut me down, or y'all here to question my girls?"

"Maybe on another visit we'll inquire about their ages," Zack said.

"Okay." Nasty pointed. "Go through those curtains right there, and then there's a door. It's unlocked. That's their dressing room."

As they entered the dressing room, most of the girls were calling it a night, packing their costumes in bags and small suitcases. It was two in the morning, and the last dancer was on stage. The dressing room could rival any in Vegas. There were countless sitting stools, each with twenty-by-twenty mirrors and multiple light bulbs around them, which allowed the girls to primp and preen themselves. Several strippers walked buck naked, and a few times, Zack's eyes followed them as they walked by.

"Damn." Zack faked a wistful sigh. "I've died and gone to heaven. Don't wake me up."

Kim nudged him and jokingly said, "Keep it up. You won't get none of this anymore."

"Okay, back to business. We are looking for Maria. Let's try to find her tonight."

"You said she was blonde. Or maybe she wears a blonde wig."

"Yeah."

"I've seen about four girls that look like that."

They settled on one blonde that was wiggling into a pair of leotards.

"Excuse me, Miss," Zack asked. "Are you Ms. Maria?"

"Yes. That would be me." She continued to get dressed and was now putting on her sneakers. "You guys must be the cops that's been poking around here tonight."

"Oh, you knew," Zack said.

"Yes, news travels fast in this place. So you guys wanted to know about the johns that give big tips?"

"Yep."

"Well, there are several."

"So what does this guy look like?"

"He was fifty-something with thinning brown hair. A little chubby."

"Was? He's dead?" She asked excitedly.

"Yes."

"That description sounds like Mr. Big Time or Mr. Vegas. He shows up mostly on the weekends."

"Mr. Vegas?" Zack asked.

"Damn." She sighed. Then there was a long pause. "It's gotta be Mr. Big Time. He owned a lot of real estate."

Kim noticed how her demeanor changed. "You seem very sad. Were you guys close?"

"No. Maybe somewhat." She caught herself before uttering, "He was really a good tipper."

"Was he like that with the other girls?" Kim asked.

"Some. But not all." Caitlyn reflected. "I was his favorite. He always made it rain when I danced."

"So did you guys have something going on?" Kim went on.

"No, he always gave me nice tips. That's all."

"You never had anything to do with him outside the club?" Zack inquired.

Kim chimed in. "You didn't have a reason to kill him, did you?"

"C'mon now." Maria rolled her eyes at her. "Please. Why would I kill the goose laying the golden egg? I heard, just like I said, news spreads fast here. That Skylar Hicks ratted me out. She doesn't like me, but that's her problem." There was a short pause. "I'm pretty sure y'all heard from the other strippers that he and his wife had an open marriage." She checked herself. "Well, sorta. But anyway, that was their thing. It didn't have anything to do with me. I believe he had problems long before he started coming here."

"Do you own any guns?"

"Nope." Then she yawned. "It's been a long night. I'm tired. It's late. I hope I was able to help you guys."

Zack said, "Somewhat, but I'd still like to ask a few more things. Here's my card."

Chapter 24

Mayor Brownlow was partying at a motel in Virginia Beach with two naked young women when his cell beeped. He had just snorted three lines of cocaine through a rolled-up hundred-dollar bill when he leaned over to peek at his cell display on the nightstand.

Brownlow answered the phone with a scowl. "Damn, Tad. I told you not to call me unless it was an emergency."

"I … I." Tad managed to stutter.

"What!" Brownlow barked, pushing away one of the high girls rubbing on his inner thigh.

Stammering again, Tad continued. "I … I wouldn't have called you, but when I was in your office, the governor had left you a message."

"Is that right?" Brownlow's anger dropped a few notches.

"The governor was very upset. Of course, he asked where you were," Tad said.

"What did you tell him?" Brownlow asked.

"That you were at Virginia Beach for the weekend."

"Why did you have to tell him that?" Brownlow asked. "You could have told him I was around town or something. Why did he call?"

Tad replied, "He asked what the hell was going on in Tilton. There's been three murders in a short time, and nothing's been done about it."

Brownlow again said, "Is that right?"

"Yeah, that's right," Tad replied. "The governor said the feds are sending an FBI agent from the field office down in Richmond to help solve these cases. He said a scathing article written by a journalist from the *Richmond Times and Dispatch* who visited Tilton to see what was going on disturbed him. He paraphrased that the journalist said in the piece about how such a small, blue-collar town could have a high number of killings. And that the police department and city leaders aren't even close to solving them."

"Well." Brownlow sighed as this revelation had tamped down his high a little. "I'll get Chief Watts on it when I get back."

"It better be soon." Tad added.

"What's that supposed to mean?" Brownlow asked as one of the girls climbed into his lap.

"There's going to be a press conference at ten tomorrow morning to discuss what's going on with these unsolved killings," Tad said. "So you might want to cut your trip short."

"Okay, I'll be there."

When Brownlow ended his call, the girls had made five long, neat lines of cocaine on the mirror for him to snort. He didn't disappoint them. Brownlow quickly inhaled the white stuff through his nostrils and lay back against the headboard to let it settle in his brain. Over the next two hours, he and his two companions partied hard, drinking Hennessy and Coronas and having a ménage à trois.

Brownlow hit the highway at four in the morning, heading back to Tilton.

———⟫●⟪———

It was a hot September day, but a gentle breeze had stirred up, which made the morning temperature bearable. Satellite trucks from several major networks, like CNN, ABC, FOX, and other media outlets, were already in front of the police station steps, having set up their equipment two hours earlier.

And just outside the entrance of the station beyond the double-glassed doors was a concrete landing where multiple microphones sat atop an impromptu podium. Surrounding the podium in a semicircle fashion was a line of metal folding chairs.

A gaggle of news reporters and curious onlookers waited impatiently, glancing at their watches from time to time and wondering when the mayor and top brass from the police department would come out and address the media. It was ten thirty, way past the time the press conference was supposed to start.

Suddenly, Mayor Brownlow came through the double-glassed doors, followed by Assistant Mayor Conway, Chief Watts, Detective Townes, and other high-ranking members of the police force.

Brownlow walked up to the mics. "I would like to thank everyone for coming." He paused for a beat. "Let me get to why we are here. Yes, there have been three murders in a very short time. We will get to the bottom of these killings and bring this monster to justice." He brought out a handkerchief from his shirt pocket to sneeze. As he did, blood was on the handkerchief. "Damn." His eyes bulged as he stepped from the mics. "Excuse me while Chief Watts gives a statement."

"Are you okay?" Chief Watts asked the mayor, giving him a pat on the back.

Brownlow nodded that he was all right. But at the time, he didn't really know because the more he blew, the more his nose bled. Then he waved for the assistant mayor to fill in for him as he went inside the station.

Chapter 25

A black female FBI agent from the field office out of Richmond was called in to assist with the homicides. Agent Becky Tally's complexion was so light that most people thought she was white. And that included Kim and Zack. The thirty-something woman with closely cropped hair was very attractive. She had hazel eyes, and a great body accented her appeal. She had won numerous beauty contests in her younger years, but the judges told her that she could never be Miss Virginia because she was too short. She was just shy of five feet. But the wins she managed to get helped her financially while attending Old Dominion in Norfolk. She hit the books hard as a double major in psychology and criminology.

She always used her mother's sayings to guide her through life. For instance, when she was informed she could never be Miss Virginia, her mother said, "Pretty is what pretty does. Your looks can take you but so far. It fades as you get older, so have a career where you can be self-sufficient and never have to depend on someone else." Becky regarded those sayings as tenets as she went about her daily life.

Zack and Kim were poring over photos and files of the deceased when Agent Tally rapped on the door. She was wearing a navy polo shirt, khakis, and a blue jacket with "FBI Agent" stenciled on the front pocket and back. They both turned and looked up at her.

"Agent Tally out of Richmond." Becky walked in and extended her hand.

The detective stood up from behind his desk. She leaned back to take all of the big man in.

"Lieutenant Zack Townes, ma'am."

"I'm so glad you're on our side." Her small paw disappeared into his mitten. "So how tall are you?'

He laughed. "Between six-six to six-eight. That's depending if my back isn't acting up and I can stretch all the way out."

Kim coughed as she stood up.

Becky turned to shake her hand. "Oh, I'm sorry. Agent Tally."

Zack motioned at a chair. "Have a seat, Agent Tally."

"Call me Becky." Once everybody was seated, Becky said, "I'm here to help out. Nothing more. Hopefully, the resources I'm able to bring to bear would facilitate you all in catching the culprit or culprits. At the moment, we don't know if there's one or two."

"Good," Zack said. "In the past, this police department hasn't had the greatest relationship with the feds. Not to get on my soapbox, but they always come in very arrogantly and basically push us to the side to snag all the glory, if there's any. And then they leave town like they are some type of damn superhero. Pardon my French."

"I know what you mean. I get this all the time when I come in. There are some agents, I hate to say it, that are like that. Your feelings are understandable. But I'm different. I'm a facilitator. I'm not here to be a pain in the butt or steal someone's thunder."

Zack told her about all three murders. Zack described Cohen and his unfortunate emasculation.

Becky's eyebrows went up. "What? Penis cut off. That's very personal stuff. If they are connected, we might have a female serial killer on our hands."

"Isn't that rare?" Kim asked.

"Absolutely," Becky replied. "Aileen Wuornos was the last well-known one. But this chick has a little of Lorena Bobbitt in her."

"Damn, those names just came to your mind easily." Zack laughed. "We caught hell trying to come up with them."

"That's because I deal with the sickos on a daily basis, and many don't make the national news."

Zack stretched. "Well, team, let's get to work on solving these cases."

Chapter 26

The next morning, Agent Tally gave her presentation to the whole police department. When nearly everybody was seated, the gathering group was mainly cops, a few social workers, and clinicians.

"Good morning, everyone." Becky peered around the room in her catlike glasses. She was garbed in a navy pantsuit that accentuated her hourglass figure and a pair of white Nikes on her feet. "The killer definitely has his or her own agenda. He or she has no empathy for the victims he or she kills because he or she is cold as ice. Most of the time, they hide in plain sight. Ordinary people like you and I. But that what's make killers like them so elusive."

Before she could utter another word, a cop raised his hand. She nodded toward a male cop.

"You think it could be a woman?"

"Absolutely."

"How so?"

She chuckled. "Years ago when I worked in Miami and Dade County, I and a few colleagues just knew our perp was a man because each one of the victims, similar to a few of these, died from strangulation. A woman wouldn't have had the strength, but she did. We later found out after catching her that she had been a power lifter in college and almost made the Olympic team as such. So I never rule out a female or anybody for that matter, even someone with a handicap."

The FBI agent cleared her throat and started again. "This person possibly had a very troubled upbringing, maybe mentally and/or physically abused. Over the years of doing this type of work, I have dealt with numerous criminals in jail, and almost to the letter, they would say they were abused in some manner when they were a child. We all know that a baby needs nurturing, to be loved and cared for. But if someone is vicious and mean toward him or her and this persists over time, that child will begin to have a very skewed or twisted outlook on life.

"Let's take Gary Ridgway, the Green River Killer, for example. He's the most prolific serial killer this country has ever seen. He killed forty-plus women. His father abused him as a child, mentally and physically. We at the Bureau believe his hatred for women stems from when he rode with his father as a bus driver for the Seattle Transit system. His father worked late at night, and prostitutes would get on board. He would tell his young son they were the scum of the earth and didn't deserve to live.

"Even though his father was married to Gary's mother, he would on many occasions pull over to the side of the road and have sex with one of them in front of his son. Talk about hypocrisy. To reiterate, many experts, psychologists and psychiatrists alike, believe that's when the seed of hatred was planted with Ridgway.

"Another disturbing sign with him was with his mother. She wore very provocative clothing, trying to look younger than her age. And because he was a bed-wetter as a teenager, she made it her business to give him a complete bath. He claimed it wasn't incestuous, but his feelings for her crossed the line. At any rate, it definitely was inappropriate and deviant."

Becky stopped. "Any questions?"

There weren't any. They all exited the conference room.

Chapter 27

Zack was on the road when his cell rang. He grabbed it from the middle console between the front seats. He kept his eyes on the road, groped for it, and quickly glanced at the display screen. It was Kim.

"What's up?" he asked.

"Do you know where Kathy is?" Kim asked.

"Yeah, at school, isn't she?"

"No. She was just picked up for prostitution. The vice squad caught her downtown in her hooker outfit."

"What?" This had to be some sort of bad joke. Only Kim wouldn't go there. No one would. No, it had to be a mistake. "I'll be right down to straighten this up."

"All right."

They hung up. Zack headed straight for the police station.

Kathy was in a holding cell. Her face was all dolled up with makeup. She was wearing a white halter top that exposed her midriff. A plain miniskirt was so short that the red panties were showing. And to accentuate the rest of her body were black fishnet stockings and a pair of Manolo stilettos.

Zack glared at her. Shock and disgust set in. "Look at you. You look like a two-bit—" He caught himself. Looking around, he saw a coat on a coat rack. "Cover your damn self up. What's wrong with you?" Zack was seething as he scooted a chair in front of her. He stared her straight in the eye, the same approach he used doing his interrogations.

She just shrugged her shoulders and then finally said, "Maybe you don't really know me."

Zack wanted to respond immediately, to scream, "What the hell are you talking about?" That would have been his natural instinct, but he caught himself again. Maybe he didn't know her especially acting like this. But he definitely didn't want his own flesh and blood to be a damn hooker, a whore, someone out on streets selling her ass for money.

He was gazing into her eyes, the same eyes she took from her mother, the ones that captured his heart so many years ago. "So tell me what I'm missing."

Their eyes locked. Kathy's lips quivered. Her eyes began to well up. Zack felt her pain. Tears rolled down both of their eyes. They embraced.

"I love you, Dad."

"I love you, too, sweetie," Zack said while still hugging her. He whispered in her ear, "What happened to my little girl?"

"I'm here. Sort of."

They released each other, wiped away their tears, and laughed.

His tone turned serious again, "Help me to understand, sugar. What am I missing?"

With her little girl charm that always used to melt his heart, she tilted her head and cocked an eyebrow. "Do you really want to know, Dad?"

"Absolutely."

She paused a second and then started. "I tried to tell you when we first moved in the new house."

"Okay, okay."

"I don't want to get into it with you, Dad. But when we were growing up, you weren't there for us."

Zack cut her off. "Hold up! Hold up! So it's about that again."

"Yes, sir. That's if you care to listen," she said pleadingly.

"Go ahead."

"Dad, I wanted a hug. I wanted a story. I wanted to be tucked in at night."

She was getting to him. He stood up, took a deep breath, and rubbed his bald, shiny head in frustration, all the while staring into her eyes.

His daughter continued. "To protect me." Her tone shifted a little. "And then there were the missed birthdays and holidays."

"Stop it! Stop it! Stop it now!" he screamed. "You're trying to make me feel bad. And you are doing a damn good job. But I did send the cards and money. I paid my child support."

"Money and cards were nothing. I didn't want some damn card. I wanted you. I cried many nights, hoping you'd come."

"Not to diminish what you are saying, but you had a mother. Where was she?"

Kathy glared at him. "Mom's only concern was money. She always wanted to wear the best. The best shoes, the best clothes, diamonds. Always dated what she called 'up', any man that was higher up on the social ladder, from businessmen, professors, doctors, and lawyers. You name them, she was always moving up to greener pastures."

Zack chuckled. "You don't have to remind me. I know firsthand how things turned out the way they did for us. I could never please her financially. I am sorry you feel that way, sweetie. I can't change the past, but I can try as hard as I can to be the best father today that I can be."

She waited a beat, gazed into his eyes, stood up, and hugged him. "Fair enough, Dad."

"You know I can lock you up for prostitution. Plus, you are underage as well."

"Wouldn't that get you in trouble?"

"Maybe somewhat. But I'll see what I can do about getting those charges dropped."

"Okay."

"That doesn't mean you're off the hook." He sighed. "And I guess neither am I."

Chapter 28

Stockton Hills was an upscale neighborhood. Each property was worth at least a quarter of a million dollars. Chuck Stewart had gotten rich off real estate long before the housing market collapsed in 2008. He started out as a slumlord, owning several run-down trailer parks and a slew of shabby houses around the poor areas of the city. As time went on, he sold his slum property for a hefty profit, and he began to buy up middle-class homes and rent them out to section 8 clients. Before long, his thriving real estate business elevated him to a higher tax bracket and a very wealthy lifestyle.

Zack had called Chuck Stewart's wife, Ruby, earlier and said he was on his way over. He rang the doorbell and heard footsteps approaching the door. And when the door opened, a thin, tall woman around fifty, with sandy brown hair greeted him.

"Come on in, Detective Townes."

He shook her hand before he stepped into the spacious foyer. A huge chandelier hung from the ceiling, and a winding staircase ascended somewhere upstairs. The opulence wasn't anything to Zack. Over the years, he had seen many a mansion, and this one was no different. She motioned for him to enter the parlor to the right. The space was very cozy and held Queen Anne furniture.

"You have a very nice place here, Mrs. Stewart."

She sighed. "Yeah, everything isn't as it seems."

A beam of light from the sun shone through the open drapes onto Mrs. Stewart's face. Along with the worry marks around her mouth were two huge sad eyes.

"Can you elaborate on that point for me, Mrs. Stewart?"

"Sure. But call me Ruby."

"Okay."

She was about to start but paused. Her face clouded up, and her eyes brimmed with tears. Then a beat later, she spoke, "Chuck could at times be the most charming husband in the world. But there's always the 'but,' you know. So, I'm not surprised the bastard was killed."

Zack's eyebrows rose. "You didn't kill him, did you?"

Ruby laughed. "At one time, I probably would have killed the bastard, but I thought long and hard about the consequences. He wasn't worth it."

"Okay," Zack said, not knowing whether to believe her or not.

"He was the most coldhearted SOB I ever met."

"What?" Zack asked. "And why would you say that?"

"He always told me that, when I got married to him, if he ever got wealthy, he would buy me all the worldly possessions a woman would want. But I had to let him live the type of lifestyle he wanted."

"That's kind of weird, and you married him anyway?" Zack asked with a wrinkled brow. "So, I gather you guys had an open marriage?"

"No, not on my end."

"Obviously, he thought you guys did."

"Yeah, I guess," she said. "I didn't take his little statement seriously. But the next thing I knew, he was bringing young girls into the house. He would screw those whores in the guest bedroom and wake up the next day like nothing happened."

"Were the girls eighteen or older?"

"I'd hope so, but barely."

"So why didn't you leave?"

"The short answer is that he wouldn't let me. Once when I had my bags packed, he pulled a gun on me. He pressed it into my face and said, 'You are not going to destroy me by getting half of my wealth.'"

"Sounds like no prenup when you guys got married."

"That's right." Ruby explained. "When we first met, we were teachers living in a modest apartment. And we came up with a plan to pool our money and buy some cheap houses. Fix them up, and rent them out. Within a short few years, we began to make some real money. You know a teacher's salary isn't all that much."

"So you guys started out jointly."

"At first, yes. But I kept working as a teacher, in part for the health benefits. Chuck quit teaching, dedicated his time toward the business, and sort of lost his damn mind when the money started rolling in."

"Back to those young girls, did he solicit sex from prostitutes?"

"You know, to be quite honest with you, I wouldn't put it past him. Chuck was a sex addict."

"Did you guys have any children?"

"Yes, a son. Chuck Junior. He's a grad student at Dartmouth. Nothing like his father. Thank God."

"Is there anything else you'd like to tell me, Ruby?"

She paused for a moment. "Chuck had enemies."

"Like whom?"

"Well, he always butted heads with a couple of his contractors. He didn't pay them like he should have. Oftentimes, they would call the house, complaining to me. I'd tell them that I had nothing to do with it. Most of them had to hunt him down to get paid."

"Sounds like he was cheap."

"Not cheap. Just greedy. It left more money for him and his damn whores."

"Speaking of them, did he have a problem with any of them?"

"How would I know? I'd see them go in and out the house. Sometimes they would flip me the bird or make childish faces when passing. And at other times, they'd call here. I'd answer the phone and hang up on them. I sure as hell wasn't going to get chummy with them."

"He didn't have a cell phone?"

"Of course he did."

"Why would they call the landline?"

"You should ask him." She smirked. "Oh, I forgot. The dog is dead."

"You really hated the guy."

She paused and reflected. "You know, at one time, I really, truly loved that man. But when he pulled that gun on me and rubbed those bitches in my face ..."

Zack just shrugged. "One last thing."

"Okay."

"Of those women he dated, was there one who came here more than the others did?"

Ruby thought for a second. "Yes, a tall blonde with blue eyes. I did see her more often than the rest."

"Thanks."

The detective thought, while pulling out the driveway, he still couldn't rule out Ruby because he didn't have the murder weapon. She was on his radar as a person of interest.

Kim was sitting at Zack's desk, staring at the laptop computer screen, when Zack walked in. "How did things go with Mrs. Stewart?"

He went over the coffee machine to fix himself a cup. He took a deep breath after dropping three lumps of sugar into the black brew, stirring it, and then taking a sip.

"Mr. Stewart loved young women. He didn't mind splurging on them, as we can attest to from Ms. Skylar Hicks."

"I knew that, Zack." Kim scribbled something down with her eyes locked on the computer screen. "But did his wife know that? And if so, what did she think of his behavior?"

Zack chuckled as he took a seat in a folding chair. "Actually, she's relieved. Said the bastard got what he deserved. She claimed he threatened her with a gun if she tried to leave him."

Kim cut him off. "I got it. So, she couldn't get half."

"Yup."

"A typical man who's so afraid his wife is going to get what he has. Hell, they are partners. She deserves her share."

"Hey, don't put me in that category." Zack threw up his hands and then took another sip of coffee. "What are you writing down?'

"Somebody's been using Mr. Stewart's credit cards. They have been very active. They also have been withdrawing his money from an ATM as well."

Zack got up from the chair. "Let's check it out, partner."

Chapter 29

Some of the purchases were at several clothing stores at the mall. Zack and Kim chatted with the cashier on duty that day at Foot Locker.

She said, "It was three young men. They looked to be teenagers: two black and one white. They spent over $1,000 on Jordans."

"How were they acting?" Kim inquired.

"At first, timid. The leader, I presume, a tall, skinny black guy who did most of the talking and taking charge, gave me the black Visa. Not to be judgmental, but I felt like they couldn't afford a card like that. I see the well-to-do, preppy kids use them all the time. They didn't look or dress like them. Another thing, when they had the Jordans in their possession, they were giving each other high fives."

"Anything else you can tell us?" Zack asked.

"No, other than they left here and went over to Neiman Marcus."

They thanked her, left, and headed over to Neiman Marcus. A similar scenario had occurred there. It didn't take long to run up a tab in such a high-end store. And when they left, they had spent $4,000.

"We need to get them on tape," Zack asked Kim. "Where's the security officer?"

They both looked around.

"There he is." Kim pointed at a stout, elderly man in a black uniform.

They introduced themselves and asked if they could see the mall's surveillance recording.

"Sure thing, guys," he said. "Just follow me."

After taking two escalators to the bottom floor, all strolled into a room with a bank of video cameras, twenty to be exact, of every angle of the inside and outside of the establishment.

"You guys need it for today?" The security officer was ready to punch in the date on a keyboard.

"No, not today," Zack said. "It was two days ago."

"Okay." The security officer put in the date. "What time?"

"We don't know the time, sir," Zack said. "But can you go to the camera where Foot Locker and Neiman Marcus is located and fast forward, and I'm pretty sure we will find what we are looking for."

"No problem."

Within minutes, the three boys were on tape, giggling, fist-bumping, and giving each other high fives as they clung to the new merchandise.

"Little thieves," Kim whispered, staring at the screen.

"Can you zoom it in a little closer?" Zack asked.

"Sure."

"That tall, scrawny kid looks familiar, Kim"

"He sure does." She leaned toward the screen.

"That's what's-his-name?" Kim was trying to come up with his name. "You know, the one that got kicked out of high school for bringing a gun to class. Said he would bust a cap in his teacher for failing him."

"Tashawn Jackson," Zack said.

"That's him," Kim said.

They thanked the security officer and made a quick exit out the building.

On their way to Tashawn's mother's home, Kim turned to Zack. "Zack?" Kim asked with a spark in her eye, peering over at him as he drove.

"Yes."

"Do you remember what caliber of gun he had?

Zack smiled. "It was a .380."

"That's right." Kim laughed. "So you think he's the killer?"

"You know, he could very well be him, but it doesn't match the profile."

"Maybe the profile's wrong," she said.

"Could be," he said, but he doubted it.

The double-wide trailer was set among ranch-style brick homes. In the front yard were children's toys. Parked next to the trailer were two cars, a silver Altima and a tricked-out Impala with shiny wheels. They parked and made their way up the small flight of stairs onto the porch. Kim rang the doorbell.

Angela Jackson, a brown-skinned, fortyish woman with rollers in her hair, opened the door. "Officer Townes and Patterson, what is it this time?"

"May we come in?" Zack asked.

"Be my guest." She opened the door wide and waved them in. "Have a seat."

"No, thank you," Kim said. "This shouldn't take long."

"Is Tashawn here by any chance?" Zack asked.

"I don't know," Mrs. Jackson said. "Tashawn!"

Tashawn appeared with a baby girl in his arms. "Yeah. What?" He looked surprised to see Townes and Patterson, two people he was quite familiar with. "What y'all want?"

They eyes went straight to the new pair of sneakers he was wearing.

"Where did you get those Jordans?" Kim asked.

"The store, like everybody else."

Zack chimed in. "How did you pay for them?"

"With money."

"Whose money?" Zack asked.

"My damn money, cop!" Tashawn snapped.

Zack got tired of the little game. "That's a damn lie. You little thief. Mall security cameras caught you and two other punks buying Jordans and other things with a dead man's credit card."

Tashawn put down the child. Then he turned his gaze at his mother, giving her a disappointing look.

"Tashawn, Tashawn," she said with her voice cracking. "You said you'd be good. Why? Why you won't do right?" She slapped him across his head. "Get your shit, and get out of here."

"But, Mom," he said with slouching shoulders, "I didn't see nothing wrong with it. Hell, besides, they just said he was dead. He'd never know."

"Y'all arrest his stupid ass. Boy, get the hell out of my face."

Zack added. "Maybe not right now, Angela."

"What else did you guys steal?" Kim asked.

"Some cash, his shoes, and the rings off his fingers."

"Bunch of vultures." Angela cut her eyes at her son.

"Did y'all steal a gun?" Kim asked.

"No," Tashawn said.

"One like you brought onto school property a while back." Zack added.

"Nope. We saw no gun."

"Do you still have that .380?" Zack asked.

"Yeah."

"Where is it?"

"It's in my car, under the driver's seat. I'll get it for y'all."

"Under the seat is a concealed weapon charge," Kim said.

"C'mon, man." Tashawn led them out of the trailer. "Cut me some slack."

He handed the weapon over to Zack, and the detective wrapped it in a white handkerchief he pulled out of his shirt pocket.

"When was the last time you shot it?"

"About a year ago."

"I'll give you a break right now with the stealing and use of stolen credit cards. But it will depend on the results from ballistic testing. If there's a match, we will be back and charge you for everything, including the killing of Mr. Stewart."

"All right."

"But before I let you go," Zack said, "where is the credit card and rings?"

Tashawn handed over two rings and the credit card.

Chapter 30

For many years, Zack always liked to keep up with the latest news on the street. He relied on several informants. His longtime, main informant, Willie Bobo, had died, and Fast Eddie replaced him. He was so named because he moved and talked fast. There was a nervousness about him. He always looked over his shoulder and from side to side when he talked, as if someone were after him. Being a petty thief, he never committed any serious crimes that would send him to the big house. Plus, with his scrawny frame, he wouldn't last there long anyway.

If Eddie wasn't on the street corner hawking something he had stolen, he was shooting craps or hustling somebody on the pool table. After he rounded the corner and didn't see him, Zack parked, got out of the cruiser, and headed for the pool hall down the alley.

As he drew near the place, he could hear a loud roar as people inside were cussing and laughing. When he entered, a wall of smoke, musk, and alcohol met him. The air was so tinged with smoke that it gave the place a foggy appearance. Nearly everybody in the pool hall had abandoned the other tables and surrounded the prominent one in the middle of the room. The patrons were so engaged in the game that they didn't notice Zack when he stepped in.

On the apron of the pool table was a small pile of money. Two men were competing for the stack of cash. Fast Eddie, seemingly only a little bigger than the pool stick, was chalking up, and his rival, a young man in his twenties, slightly chubby with dreadlocks, was leaning across the table and about to strike the cue ball. And when he did, he scratched. Eddie's eyes grew large. The pool table was half-full of balls.

"Watch this," said an old onlooker to the guy sitting beside him. "He's going to run the damn table."

Before Eddie started, he nodded over at Zack. "Watch this, big man. Six ball in this pocket." He pointed with the pool stick.

With the greatest ease, skill, and confidence, he did run the table. When the cue ball struck the other balls, they damn near jumped off the pool table as they flew into the leather pockets with a bang. There were laughs and a few sour faces all around. Eddie gathered up the stacks and then shook Dreadlocks's hand. Several people congratulated him with pats on the back.

Zack made his way over. "Damn, Eddie, you have some skills."

They shook hands.

"Yeah, everybody tells me that. And that it's my calling. I guess I'm pretty good."

"I must say. Who knows, you might be the next Minnesota Fats. He started out as a hustler."

"That right?" Eddie then changed to a serious tone. "I know why you are here."

"Yup. I need some street info."

"Okay, let's sit over there in that corner next to the window. I'll be over in a second. Want a beer?"

"Sure."

"What kind? It's on me."

"Corona."

"Okay, I'll be right back."

Zack lit up a Newport and gazed out the window overlooking the river that ran through the middle of town. Almost half of the businesses on the riverfront were boarded up since the recession of 2008.

Eddie headed to the table with two chilled bottles of Corona. After a sip of the Corona, Eddie whispered, "Word on the street is that a black tattoo artist is somehow connected to the Mexican mob."

Zack asked, "Is that right?" He took a long pull from the Newport and took a swallow of beer. "So you think he had something to do with the truck driver's murder?" The detective snubbed out one Newport and quickly lit another one with his Bic.

Eddie was squirrel-like as he peered around before answering, "I don't know."

"Is he a drug dealer or something?"

"Man, like I said, I don't know. Might be."

There was a short silence.

"They say the guy pretty much got the tattoo thing sewed up around town," Eddie said.

"Is that right?" Zack replied.

"Yeah. A couple of his competitors had to shut down. He took their business."

"Don't tell me they came to you and snitched on him, saying he's pushing drugs."

"Actually I heard that through the grapevine."

"Maybe they're upset and lying about him."

Eddie shrugged. "Grapevine's grapevine. If you want absolute truth, go to church."

They both finished their Coronas, and Zack was getting the last drag from his Newport and then putting it out in a tin ashtray.

"Where's his shop?" Zack asked.

"It's right off South Avenue and Vine. Guy's name's Ahmad Ali."

"Arab?"

"Naw. Black Muslim, I think."

Over the years, Zack had run into quite a few blacks who had converted to Islam. Most had joined the Nation of Islam, a national Muslim sect led by Louis Farrakhan.

They stood up to leave. Zack reached into front pocket, pulled out a crumpled twenty, and gave it to Eddie.

Eddie looked at the twenty and licked his lips. "One more thing, Zack. They say most of Mr. Ali's customers are women, especially strippers."

That was interesting. Zack tossed him another five.

"Today must be my lucky day." Eddie was smiling. "Thanks."

<hr />

Ali Ahmad's tattoo shop was downtown between a boutique and a barbershop. It was a very narrow space. Zack could almost touch the walls on both sides. He figured it could have been no more than ten feet across because his wingspan was seven feet.

When he walked in, he gave the place a cursory look. Crowded on the walls were pictures of multiple people, men and women alike, he obviously had tatted. As he ambled farther into the shop, a young, light-skinned woman was getting a tat on her lower back.

The tattoo artist, he presumed, was Mr. Ali. He had huge magnifying glasses on his eyes, and had his back to him.

Flashing his badge, Zack asked, "Are you Ahmad Ali?"

Ahmad paused for a moment, turned around slightly, looked at Zack, and then continued what he was doing. "That's the name on the door."

Zack didn't care for the smart remark. The artist was working on a heart with a green snake wrapped around it. The girl Ahmad was working on was facing the detective and snickered.

"I need to ask you a few questions," Zack said.

"Go ahead," Ahmad said, still into his work.

Zack was getting angry. "Mr. Ali, sir, can you take a break for a few seconds?"

Ahmad sighed and carefully laid the bloody tattoo machine on a red cloth. "All right."

Ahmad looked to be about forty. He was a small man, around five-two, with a brown complexion. He had tats that seemed to cover every inch of his body from his neck all the way down, and he wore a white wifebeater.

"I'm investigating the murder of Roger Tuck."

Ahmad just shrugged.

"I believe you did tats on him and his girlfriend."

"Officer," Ahmad said, trying to remember his last name.

"Townes."

"Officer Townes, I've done hundreds, if not thousands, of tats, so you'll have to be more specific."

"Well, theirs were Cupid shooting an arrow. They matched." Zack looked around the wall to see if theirs were up there. He stopped after scanning for thirty seconds. "Right there." He pointed his finger. "That's them."

Ahmad studied the photo. "Oh, yeah. I remember them. An odd couple. At first, I thought he was her father, you know, with the age gap and all. But when they were all lovey-dovey, then I knew that they were probably going together."

Zack thought about what Fast Eddie had said about Ali being in the drug trade. He wondered how to ask him about it without Ali clamming up. He might not want to discuss it. So he was going to use a different tactic.

"If you haven't heard," Zack said, "Mr. Tuck's a head short."

"Is that right?" Ahmad said in mock surprise.

"You don't seem too surprised."

"I read the news," Ahmad said.

Zack said, "It's rumored some Mexicans did it."

Ahmad shrugged.

"Have you tattooed some of them?"

"Killers or Mexicans?" Ahmad asked.

"Don't be a wiseass," Zack said.

"A few Latinos came by not too long ago. Didn't catch their country of origin though."

"I hope you took pictures of them."

"They weren't my type."

Zack sighed. "I meant the tats."

"Yeah," Ahmad said. "I know what you meant."

"So?"

"Sure. I was proud of that project because it was different."

The young woman was getting restless as she switched her position. "Damn, Ali, hurry up. I'm getting cramps, man."

"Okay, okay," he said hurriedly. "I need to get back to my client." But before turning back to his work, Ahmad quickly surveyed the many pictures again. He pointed at a photo. "There they are. Like I said, it was unique. Difficult, too, but I pulled it off."

The photo was of three young Mexican men looking over their shoulders with their backs to the camera, flashing gang signs. Tatted on their backs were huge skulls and crossed bones with "Zeta and Sinola Posse" etched across it. *Bingo.*

The detective felt they had to be the killers or they knew damn well who was. He took out his smartphone. "I need to take a picture of them with my cell."

"Go right ahead." Ahmad went back to working on the woman.

Zack zoomed in and got a good shot of the three, snapping it. He put the cell back in his pocket. "One last thing before I leave."

"Shoot."

"You aren't selling drugs, are you?"

"Hell naw," Ahmad said. "The prophet says your body is a temple. I don't pollute his temple."

Zack looked at the born-to-ride tattoo right above the girl's ass. He wondered what the prophet would say about that. "Well, I heard you might."

"Sounds like those jealous fools that I put out of the tat business. I can't help that they couldn't compete with greatness."

Zack smiled.

Chapter 31

Zack, Kim, and Becky were in the detective's office, going over the three killings, when the dispatcher, a heavyset black woman in her fifties, tapped on the open door.

"There's another killing,"

All eyes turned toward her as she stood inside the threshold of the door.

"Where?" Zack asked.

"North Tilton at Slidell apartments." The dispatcher sighed. "I believe it's another male."

"Okay, thanks." Zack stood. "Are you riding with us, Becky?"

"Sure," Becky said.

Twenty minutes later, they were at the crime scene. Two uniforms were posted a few feet beyond the yellow police tape. Zack ducked under the tape, along with Kim and Becky. Before entering the apartment, Zack stopped for a split second and gazed at the front entrance to see if there was a forced entry. The inside of the apartment was hot with the putrid smell of death that wafted through the air.

Zack gave the apartment a glimpse as he went. A skinny crime scene tech approached him and said he and his colleague were still processing the scene. But he showed Zack the vic's driver's license, Stan Drummond, a fifty-five-year-old white male.

Garbed in his footies and latex gloves, the slim tech said, "Zack, it appears that he was shot twice between the eyes. Give us thirty more minutes."

"All right." Zack peered over at the vic, sprawled on his back with eyes staring at the ceiling.

The techs wrapped up their job in less than twenty minutes as Zack and his team waited patiently outside in the hallway.

"Okay," the tech said, "it's all yours."

Zack thanked him as Kim and Becky followed him back in the apartment. All three were staring at the vic, lying naked, face-up, and staring at the ceiling.

"Looks like another sexual encounter gone wrong," Zack said.

"Sure does." Kim added. "But not as graphic."

"The perp obviously shot him through the pillow," Becky said. "To muffle the sound. There's gun residue on it and two small holes."

On the floor was a red necktie that was tied in a knot.

Zack slipped on a pair of latex gloves and picked it up. "I guess they were playing some type of game."

The stench from the decaying body was getting stronger as they neared the vic. Becky and Kim pinched their noses to cut down on the odor, but it didn't help. Flies were buzzing around and landing on his face and ears.

"How long has he been dead?" Kim asked nobody in particular.

Zack replied. "I'll say a few days."

"I'd agree," Becky said. "A dead body is at full rigor mortis after about thirty-six hours. He's definitely limp. And those blowflies can smell death up to a mile or two if the wind is blowing. However, in this case, the vic is indoors. But those damn flies, once they get a whiff of a corpse, are coming. They will find a way to get into the building."

"Damn," Kim said, "you sound like one of our forensic techs."

"As part of my training at the bureau, I had to take a few courses on forensics."

"Let's get out of this stifling place," Zack said.

Chapter 32

As Kim gathered up the kids' clothes to wash, a bag of weed dropped from Kathy's pants. Kim picked it up and checked it out. She thought that amount was more than recreational. Any amount of drug wasn't acceptable. In short order, she relayed what she found to Zack.

He was very disappointed that Kathy was doing drugs. If she were, Zack would put her in rehab and get the best treatment out there. Nothing less would be good enough for his little girl. He confronted her.

"Dad, I'd never do drugs," Kathy said.

"Why was it in the pockets of your clothes?" Zack asked.

"Well, a girl at school asked me to hold them for her."

"C'mon, Kathy. I'm a cop, remember. You can't pull that one on me."

"Honest, Dad."

"I tell you what." Zack stared into her eyes. "I got a urine test kit from work. I want you to take it."

"I'll take it. No problem."

Zack was startled by how self-assured she was.

"Want me to do it now?" Kathy asked.

"Yes," he said. "Absolutely."

"You don't play around. Do you, Pops?"

"Nope."

It was in a drawer in the kitchen. He pulled out the drawer and gave her the kit.

"Don't try to run tap water in it," Zack said.

Kathy laughed. "Damn, Dad. I'm not stupid."

"I don't know about that. Holding drugs for somebody isn't that smart."

Kathy left and went to the bathroom. Zack was hoping she was right and would pass the test. A minute later, she reappeared with a broad smile.

"I told you I'd pass."

Zack studied the results. She was right. She did pass. "Give me a hug."

They embraced.

He gave her a stern message. "Don't go around carrying drugs for other people. If they want to commit the crime, let them do the time."

"I know, Daddy. I know."

———◆———

Kathy was a good liar. Not only did she carry drugs around for other people, she used them and sold them as well. She was able to pass the urine test because she put a few drops of a new enzyme in it to alter the results. It was readily available on the streets as long as you had the right contacts.

Kathy dealt with Karen, her best friend from high school, to get her the drugs and the enzyme. Unassuming, standing-five seven and slightly chubby and wearing glasses, Karen wasn't pretty or ugly. She was just average looking. Kathy liked how personable she was, and they became best friends.

Karen quickly let her in their drug thing. Her boyfriend of the last six months was named New York. He was a bony, acne-faced kid from Queens who fancied himself as a low-level drug dealer. He went to their high school a year ago but dropped out. At first, he tried to work several low-wage jobs from flipping burgers to working at Walmart but quit. Karen thought he was cute, mature, and different from the country guys she had dated in the past. Her mother even let him stay in their home from time to time. A rumor spread around their school that Karen and Kathy had sex and sometimes orgies at her place.

On campus, they were inseparable. But things changed between them when Kathy told her that she couldn't help her and New York sell drugs anymore because her cop father busted her, regardless of the cut she got to buy her fancy and expensive clothes. Karen was so infuriated that she said they were no longer friends.

Kathy pleaded with her. She liked her a lot and wanted to remain friends. Karen said no. Her man depended on that money she brought in to live off. Kathy was a cog in his small-time operation, and if the cog were broken, he couldn't make a living. Kathy asked repeatedly why they couldn't stay friends. Karen wasn't hearing it.

The final blow was when she said, "My man comes first, and that's it."

So Kathy told her, dismissing her with the flick of her hand, "Oh, well. Nice knowing you."

But before they cut their ties, Karen made a vow to the former friend. "Bitch, you will pay. I got your number."

Kathy didn't know what she meant then. She just rolled her eyes, turned, and walked away.

Chapter 33

It was an odd day at the station. Zack had grabbed some coffee, but no one wanted to talk. Oh, sure, they said hi, but that was it. He felt like a pariah. Was it just paranoia? He had been working hard on the case. Maybe the lack of sleep was getting to him.

Zack was sitting in his cubicle, sipping a cup of coffee, and going over the evidence collected from the three murders, when his cell phone rang.

"Zack, are you standing or sitting?" Kim asked.

"Sitting." Zack knew this couldn't be good. "Why?"

"There's something on Facebook that's very disturbing."

His forehead wrinkled. "What? I'm not on Facebook, Twitter, or whatever they call the latest one, Instagram."

"I know. I know. But Kathy is."

"Damn, Kim." Zack sighed. "I know you guys don't like each other. What are you on, the Kathy watch?'

"No. Damnit, Zack. Give me some credit here."

There was a bit of a pause, and Zack regretted his words. "Look, Kim. I'm sorry I—"

"I don't hate Kathy. I'm worried about her," Kim said. "I know how much you love her. Zack, honey, she doesn't make good choices."

Zack wanted to argue, to tell her she was wrong, but he couldn't. He sighed. He'd just gotten on her about prostitution and drugs. What else could she be up to?

"What's on Facebook?"

"Is your computer on?" Kim asked.

"Yes."

"I was texted a few photos to my smartphone with Kathy, let's say, in a very compromising position."

"Compromising position," those words rolled around in his head. No father wanted to hear them attached to his daughter.

Kim said, "A fellow female officer sent them to me. I won't tell you her name right now."

"Fair enough." Zack turned his attention toward his computer. With dread in his voice, he asked, "How do I access this Facebook?"

Kim gave him her username and password so he could get online. Personally, he didn't care for any of the new interactive websites where everybody was airing out all his or her laundry, like what he or she ate or the last time he or she used the bathroom. It was just too much info. The only new technology he owned and appreciated was his smartphone. And Kim pushed him to get that. He also despised all the reality television that seemed to flood the airwaves. He wondered what had happened to our morals, but that was another issue for another day.

"I don't see anything, babe."

"Are you on Facebook?'

"Yup."

"Okay, I didn't try it myself, but she said that, once you get there, you will see a group of pictures labeled at the top as friends."

"I see that."

"Scroll through them until you see Lil Red Riding Hood."

"Hold on." Zack's pulse ticked up a beat. "Yeah, I got it."

"Click it."

And when he did, he couldn't believe his eyes. He had to lean in closer to make sure it was his little girl. His cell phone slipped out of his hand and clattered onto his desk. "Oh my God." His emotions ran the gamut from anger to sadness.

Kathy was buck naked on her knees on the edge of the bed. A small line of teenage boys was naked as well, waiting for their turn with her. She faced the camera with a smile on her face, seemingly at ease at what she was doing. Just above the pictures of Kathy in many different sexual positions was a message from Lil Red Riding Hood.

"I'm nominating this freak as the whore of the year. What do you think, viewers? I believe this cunt can win. Click the thumbs-up icon if you agree."

Zack's gaze moved to the thumbs-up sign and saw three hundred agreed while only two didn't. Bile built up in his throat. He instantly had heartburn.

"Zack! Zack! Honey, are you still there?" Kim's faint voice echoed from his desk.

Mechanically, he picked up his phone. "I'm here."

"So," Kim asked, "is it as bad as I think?"

"Worse."

He paused before continuing, rubbing his head in frustration. "She looks like a porn star, and that shit is in cyberspace forever."

Kim kept quiet. Anger flowed through him like electricity. He felt like bashing the damn computer screen.

"Who the fuck is this Lil Red Riding Hood?"

"I have no idea, but it has to be someone Kathy knew to get pictures of her like that."

"Maybe they're Photoshopped." Zack fully realized how lame it sounded.

Kim wasn't buying it. "I wish they were," she said.

She was right. He had to put his cop hat back on. "Back to the creep who put this shit out there. Any idea who it might be?"

"Like I said, it has to be somebody she knows to get shots like that."

"Is Kathy at home right now?"

"No. It's just me, Mrs. Jane, and the boys."

"All right, I'm going to talk to our computer guy here at the station and see if he could track down this asshole. And when Kathy shows up, tell her to stay put until I get there."

"Okay, I'll tell her."

Chapter 34

Kathy's cell phone was blowing up. She got calls from a lot of her friends talking about her photos. She instantly knew Karen was the culprit. Her idle threat wasn't empty anymore. She went to her cell phone, clicked on her Facebook page, and felt crushed. She was so outdone and wouldn't be surprised to see it was plastered on billboards around town.

It was nearly dusk. She had been hiding in the woods adjacent to their property for the last two hours. She was scared to go inside the house. She knew her dad wasn't there because Kim was off. He drove the patrol car to work, and it wasn't in the driveway. Now she watched nervously for his arrival. She never thought Karen would stoop so low.

Suddenly, headlights flickered through the woods. She hid behind a pine tree. Her heart skipped a beat. Her dad got out, slammed the door, marched up the small flight of stairs, and entered the house.

"Where is she?" His voice carried all the way to the woods.

Kim said something her father didn't like. He pulled out his phone. Kathy's phone rang twice before she answered it. She could see him in the lit kitchen window from the woods.

"Hello," she whispered.

"Young lady, you have a lot of explaining to do."

"I know, Daddy. I know."

"Where are you? Turning tricks," he said.

"No!" Kathy emerged now from the woods with tears rolling down her swollen cheeks.

"Where are you then?"

She could see his face now. It was red. Angry. It was also puffy. Had he been crying?

"Look out the kitchen window," she whispered into the phone.

When she got closer, the motion sensors tripped, bathing her in a harsh spotlight.

"I'm sorry, Daddy. I'm so sorry."

He stared at her for a moment. *Please, Daddy. Say something.*

His tight jaw relaxed. "Come on in, Kathy. Come in. Please tell me what's going on with you, girl."

She looked back at the woods. She could run, but a part of her didn't want to. All she wanted was to be held. All she wanted was to be his little girl again. She felt petrified, but she had to try to make this right. She forced her legs to move, one after the other. She didn't really feel them. She almost floated along, like in a dream. Only this wasn't a dream.

When she got in the house, she ran to him. He hugged her, but she could feel him hold something back. She tried to convince herself otherwise, but she knew the truth. She wasn't his little girl anymore.

For the next hour, Kathy pleaded her case to her dad and Kim, downstairs, so nobody in the house could hear their conversation. And when she was finished, he grounded her for a month. He took away her cell phone, and she couldn't even use the landline either.

Chapter 35

After the heart-to-heart talk with his daughter, Zack thought that everything was resolved. But less than a month later, she had slipped out the house when everybody as asleep and was out on the street corner. Zack had learned of her being gone when she never showed for breakfast.

Zack was livid. "I can't believe she left," he said more to himself than to Kim, who was seated next to him at the kitchen table.

The only other person missing was his mother. She was still sleeping. The boys were there in pajamas, blinking sleep from their eyes and yawning. Kim had fixed bacon, eggs, oatmeal, and coffee.

While sitting next to Zack, Kim couldn't help but sympathize with him. "Hon, you tried. That's all you can do."

Zack gazed into her eyes. "She gave me her word. She promised she wouldn't do this again."

One of the boys quickly finished his meal and excused himself from the table.

"Hon, remember when she said you really didn't know her."

He paused. "Yeah, yeah, that kind of cut me a little deep." He got up, ambled toward the kitchen window, and peered out across the lawn. "She rants about my not being there for them. You know, her and her brother."

"So it was that part that really hurt the most, I guess."

"Absolutely, of course. It wasn't like I supposed to just stop living because their mother and I didn't get along. I basically had moved on and moved out. And soon after, I started dating. I still had to work, and next thing you now, Diane, my girlfriend at the time, had a child." He wrung his hands in frustration, stammering, "I …I … I did my best." He mused a while longer. "Maybe I should have been there more in their lives."

Kim pushed herself from the table, walked over, and patted him on the back. "Zack, don't beat yourself up. We can't change the past. We learn from it and keep moving."

He sighed. Suddenly, they could hear the sound of small feet rushing up the stairs from the basement.

"Dad! Dad!" His son, Johnny, said excitedly, holding a sheet of paper. "She left a note on the counter."

"Okay, okay." Zack's heartbeat went up a few notches.

He took the piece of paper, it read, "First and foremost, I'm sorry. I know I promised to quit prostitution, but I lied. Living with your girlfriend and that whole setup with the rules wasn't for me. I'm beyond that now. I'm a woman. Again, I know I'm not considered an adult. But that's okay, too. So if you want to call this a runaway letter, feel free to do so. I know what I'm doing. I never was good at school, but I can still get what's mine. I know you guys are pulling y'all's hair out, but Dad, you don't have any idea what I'm going through. I still love you and my family. But that house wasn't big enough for two women, so I have to do what I have to do. Take care. Love, Kathy."

Zack took a deep breath and let it ease out.

Chapter 36

Maria and a few of her friends from her job, Gucci and Blonde, decided to get a bite to eat. They chose the Outback at the mall. They all were casually dressed in jeans, T-shirts, and sneakers.

It was two in the afternoon. The place was nearly empty. A black stripper, Gucci, was asking them if they had heard about their coworker, Skylar, being locked up allegedly for the Stewart murder.

As she spoke, a waitress asked if they were ready to give their orders. They said yes. Maria ordered lobster, a salad, and water while both of her friends ordered steaks, baked potatoes, and sweet teas. Gucci stopped talking and waited a bit for the waitress to leave their table.

"I heard he was found naked in the backseat of his Jag with a hole in his chest." Gucci continued.

"What?" Blonde asked with her eyebrows raised in surprise.

Gucci looked over at Maria. "Did you hear that too, Maria?"

Maria shrugged. "No, first I heard of it."

"I don't see how y'all missed it," Gucci said. "It's been in the paper and on TV."

Blonde added. "Don't worry, hon. I don't follow the news either. It's too depressing."

Maria nodded and thought about just being happy for an outing with the girls.

The moment the waitress had brought their food and drinks, Gucci glanced up at the flat-screen mounted on the wall. "That's it!" She pointed.

"Ma'am," she anxiously asked the waitress, "can you turn up the volume on the TV?"

"Sure." The waitress reached into her apron pocket, got the remote, and pointed at the TV to turn it up.

"Thank you," Gucci said.

Maria had her back to the set. She turned around to look. A young white female reporter was standing in the parking lot where the victim was found dead in his car.

"Yes, Mr. Stewart was a successful businessman in Tilton. A pillar in the community. His tragic and violent death has law enforcement a little puzzled; however, they have a suspect in custody. Before I mention her name, Homicide Detective Townes wanted us to remind the viewers that just because they've arrested a suspect doesn't mean that she is guilty. He said, 'Her DNA was found at the scene. But we need to find the murder weapon.'"

The reporter lifted her gaze from the pad. "Skylar Hicks is in custody for the murder of Mr. Stewart. She's a stripper at Naughty Women."

"Look! Look!" Gucci said excitedly. "We are famous."

Maria turned back around, not impressed. "We are infamous. At least locally."

"Girl, let me call some of our other coworkers." Gucci ignored Maria's comment.

Gucci whipped out her cell phone and started punching in numbers. Maria and Blonde looked at each, shrugged, and then began to eat their meals.

The volume on the television was still up. The mayor was talking now.

Blonde blurted, "Mayor Brownlow is one of my favorite customers. He always goes through the escort service. I guess so he can be incognito. But almost everybody at work knows about him. He's been with quite a few of the girls."

When Maria heard his voice, her legs began to shake. She brought them in tighter until they were touching each other. It didn't help. They kept shaking. Next, her hand with the fork started shaking.

Blonde noticed. "You okay, Maria?"

Maria didn't answer. She slowly turned around to glance up at the set. *It's him! It's him!* Her mind told her. *So, it was him with Nasty at the Marriott.*

Gucci was still busy talking into her cell phone. Maria turned back around. Everything was turning into a blur. Gucci was talking, and Blonde was staring at her, but she didn't hear her. She just saw her lips moving. She felt hot beads of sweat coming out of her pores. She felt dizzy, like she might pass out. Her hand went to her mouth like she might puke.

Finally, Maria grabbed her small purse. "I have to go to the bathroom."

She jumped up from the table and ran toward the ladies' room to vomit.

Maria finished throwing up her food, but she was starting to have dry heaves. A few minutes later, she came out of the stall, stumbled against the floor to the sink, and turned on the cold water full blast. She splashed water on her face. She clung tightly to the side of the sink to brace herself from falling. She remembered she still had some of her anxiety medicine, Valium, to calm her down. She frantically searched her purse for the bottle of medicine. She found it, popped the top, clumsily shook out a few in her hand, threw them into the back of her throat, and then leaned down and gulped mouthfuls of the rushing water.

It was going to take a little while before the medicine kicked in, but just the thought had calmed her somewhat. Then she took a few deep breaths and exhaled slowly. Things seemed to be coming back into focus now.

The water was still flowing fast from the faucet in the sink. She turned the knob to slow it down. On the outer rim of the sink, for the first time, she noticed her makeup and eyeliner had smeared. She looked up into the mirror. The nasty scar under her right eye that ran across her cheekbone was exposed. She leaned in closer to the mirror to get a better look.

"A sorry bastard! I will get you for this. I promise you. I will," she said through clenched teeth.

Suddenly, the bathroom door opened.

"Maria! Maria!" Blonde screamed.

She recognized Blonde's voice before she saw her. Scrambling now for her makeup, she quickly splashed some on the scar and rubbed it in the nick of time.

"There you are." Blonde smiled. "Are you okay? You had me worried out there."

Maria turned her head slightly to work on her scar.

"Yeah." She sighed. "I'll be all right. Thanks for the concern."

"What happened? Was it the lobster?"

"Yeah, yeah, some things don't agree with me. I guess I should have gotten steak like you guys. Where's Gucci?"

"That dumb ass bitch is still on the phone. She didn't even realize that you were sick. I don't think she's that bright."

"I'll agree to that."

Later that evening at her apartment, Maria was still reeling from when she heard and saw Mayor Brownlow on the flat-screen. She knew him very well. He was the nightmare that haunted her for years and wouldn't let her sleep. He was the reason she was in Tilton. Her emotions ran the gamut from sadness to relief. Now she was almost at peace.

"He's here," she repeated to herself. "No more searching."

She thought how wonderful it would be to punish the man who caused her so much pain, the so-called Mayor Ray Brownlow.

Chapter 37

Zack's mind was still reeling from Kathy running away from home. He didn't want to worry himself sick, so he felt the only way to cope with it was to pour himself into solving these murders.

Zack was still trying to figure out what happened with the Stewart murder. But first, he needed to find out what type of bullet was found at the crime scene, and whether or not the same gun was used for the Tuck and Stewart killings. He knew it was fired from a .380. So he got up from his desk and made his way toward the basement of the building where ballistics was located.

And when he entered the department, Zack saw the man he was looking for, Lieutenant Carter. He was forty-five, black, and overweight, with his belly hanging over his belt. At the moment, he was looking through the eyepiece of a microscope.

"What you got, Carter?' Zack asked as he walked toward him.

Carter was a twenty-year veteran of the police force. Standing five-nine, he had a thick grade of salt-and-pepper hair.

Carter smiled. "I knew you were coming, Zack."

"Always. Trying to put things together with those murders."

"I understand."

Carter had test-fired a .380 three times into the water tank and compared the rifling to the one found at the scene. He had the bullet that killed the vic on the metal table that he was standing in front of.

"Here's the bullet." He picked it up. "See the mushroom shape."

Zack picked up the slug and studied it. "It has to be a hollow-point or soft-point."

"It's a soft-point because a hollow-point would have spread out more, especially after it hit bones and organs."

"What about the angle of the projectile?" Zack asked.

"It was at a slight angle, not quite ninety degrees. I'd say more like eighty."

"So the shooter had the gun leveled almost straight over the top of him and pressed against his chest."

"Yes."

"He had to die instantly," Zack said. "The techs said the entry point was next to his heart."

Zack needed to confirm that part of the investigation. He reached into his front pocket and pulled out this cell. "Wait a second. Let me call the medical examiner right now." He flipped it open and punched in her digits.

Dr. Powell answered on the first ring. "Medical examiner's office. Dr. Powell speaking."

"This is Detective Townes from homicide."

"I was wondering when you were going to call."

Zack laughed. "What you got?"

"Well, the vic was shot with a small caliber bullet, just like Mr. Tuck."

"I'm at ballistics right now. It was a .380."

"Okay, okay. And when the firearm was discharged, the bullet traveled through his left chest. It went straight through his heart and shattered his left clavicle on the lower side of the shoulder blade before finally lodging into the car seat."

"So, I presume death was instantaneous."

"Pretty much. But not like a sharpshooter hitting someone in the brain stem. In this situation, he was in shock from the fatal wound. His heart pumped faster, spilling blood inside and outside the body. Of course, most of the leaking occurred outside."

"What about time of death, doc?"

"Given the contents in the stomach, liver test, and stage of rigor, he had been dead for five to six hours before the groundskeeper found him."

"Thanks, Dr. Powell."

"Sure thing."

They hung up. He also thanked Carter for the info and then headed back toward his office.

Zack was at his desk now, flipping through multiple photos of the murders from different angles. Gazing at the severed head of Tuck was ghoulish. It somewhat made his skin crawl. It reminded him of a mask at Halloween. He kept shuffling them around like a deck of cards as if that would miraculously help him solve the crimes. Then he put the photos down and thought.

For starters, he thought about the men that were shot. Both were shot with a small-caliber weapon. Next, they were middle-aged. One was white; one was black. What about motive? In the case of Tuck, he believed the motive was money. He was hauling a shipment of drugs, and his backers were probably the Zeta cartel, who had something to do with his death, given what he'd seen in El Paso and over in Juarez, Mexico.

And as far as the Stewart case, they had a potential killer in custody, Ms. Skylar Hicks. According to her interview, she admitted she was jealous because he was spending more time and money on the other girls, but she wouldn't dare kill him for that. There was physical evidence at the crime scene implicating her. But they all were circumstantial; moreover, they did not find the murder weapon.

Zack massaged his temples with the heels of his hands. He leaned back in his high-back chair and kicked up his heels on his desk. No sooner had he weaved his fingers behind his neck, than Kim walked in.

"Aren't we relaxed? Loafing on the job, I see." She laughed, holding a bag in one hand with Subway written on the side, along with a bottle of water and a Pepsi in the other.

Zack brought his feet down from the desk. "You must have read my mind. I'm starving."

"I kinda thought you might be hungry."

Police chatter was in the air, coming from the other cubicles.

"Want to eat outside?" Kim asked. "It's such a pretty day."

"Yeah, we can do that."

But before they left, a flat-screen television across the room caught their attention.

A young, black female reporter said, "It hasn't been a month, and this is the third murder. Is this a pattern? Is there a serial killer on the loose? The Tilton police department hasn't been able to solve any of these cases. Is the public safety at risk? Just a few unanswered questions we taxpayers need to be concerned with."

And with that, the reporter signed off.

Peeved now, Zack pulled his gaze from the flat-screen. "Damn, I'm trying. Give me a break."

"Let's go and enjoy our meal, Zack. We'll deal with that later." Kim grabbed him by the arm and led him out the building and toward a picnic area under a maple tree.

A slight breeze stirred up as a few autumn leaves floated in the air. It was September. The temperature was cooling down. They took a seat on a metal bench.

"What the hell's she talking about?" The detective took an angry bite from his sub.

"Nothing," Kim replied. "They are just trying for ratings. You know how that crap works."

He took another bite from his sandwich, and with a mouth full of food, he said, "I was working on my theory, and now I guess that little broadcast will up the ante."

"Always." Kim took a sip from the bottled water. "We know the drill. The mayor gets on the chief, and shit rolls downhill."

Zack reflected. "We are in a strange line of work."

Chapter 38

Zack and Kim decided to go back to the first crime scene to put themselves in the killer's or killers' shoes. They hopped into the cruiser and headed for the railroad tracks.

"Mr. Pruitt, the engineer that was passing by the night of the murder, said a group of Mexicans was beating Mr. Tuck." Zack walked around, scouring the area.

"But he never said he saw Mr. Tuck get shot or cut with a knife, now did he?" Kim asked.

"That's correct." Zack glanced over at her. "The beating probably happened about here," he said, mumbling something to himself.

Zack was like a man obsessed, pointing at the ground. "The dog found the skull right around here."

"Yes," Kim said.

"Right there." Zack pointed at an evidence marker that was still at the scene. He squatted down and ran his hands through the clammy soil, letting it filter through his fingers. "So, there has to be more physical evidence out here." He picked up several pieces of gravel and found specks of blood on the opposite side.

Kim knew he was deeply into his investigation now. She didn't want to interrupt the thoughts racing through his brain, so she walked up a small hill onto the railroad tracks. She squinted her eyes from the brilliant autumn sun as she stood on the cross ties and peered around at a clump of trees and underbrush that ran alongside the tracks.

About twenty yards to her right, something caught her attention. At first, she dismissed it. She thought the shiny object was nothing more than some aluminum foil. As she went to check it out, her heartbeat went up a notch or two the closer she got to it. A broad smile went across her face. It appeared to be a knife. Within a foot of it, she noticed a pointy, serrated knife with a wooden handle.

It has to be the other murder weapon. Kneeling to get a better look, she could see blood stains smeared on the blade and handle.

"Zack! Zack!" she screamed over her shoulder. "Honey, come here. I believe I found the other murder weapon."

Kim's screams broke the trance he was in, and he ran toward her voice. They both knelt down, smiling.

"Got your gloves on you, Kim?"

"Yep." She pulled out a pair of latex gloves from her back pocket.

"Let's hope," Zack said, "that the DNA isn't too degraded."

"Amen to that," Kim said. "We definitely need a break."

No sooner had Zack and Kim headed toward the police station, than a call from the dispatcher came across the radio. Zack shuddered. He was hoping it wasn't about his daughter. Kim looked over at him as he drove. It wasn't Kathy. They both took a collective breath.

"We have a white male dead at the Ramada Inn. He's floating face-down in the swimming pool," the dispatcher said. "The maid found him. She told the manager, and he called the station."

Zack made a U-turn and pulled into the subterranean parking lot. "I hope it's not another homicide."

Chapter 39

The dead man was floating next to the side of the pool. His toupee was clinging to his shiny skull, as it bobbed with the slight wave. Fat and short, he appeared to be in his sixties.

"I don't see any blood in the pool," Zack said. "He could have drowned."

"Maybe he had a heart attack," Kim added.

"Yeah, I bet that's probably what happened," Zack said.

In the distance, they could hear a siren wailing.

"Why's the siren blaring?" Zack said. "There's no rush. He's obviously dead and can't be resuscitated."

The noise stopped. EMTs parked and rushed out of their vehicle.

"Where is he?" A tall, skinny EMT asked the maid standing in the breezeway.

She pointed toward the pool.

"Right there, floating," Kim said.

Seconds later, the body was hefted out of the water.

"Those are odd," the EMT worker said.

"What?" Zack asked.

The EMT worker showed him several welts about the deceased's face and neck, Taser burns. Zack's heart sank.

He glanced over at Kim. "Here we go again. Looks like another homicide."

"It sure does," Kim replied.

Zack whipped out his cell phone and speed-dialed the forensics department. "I believe we have another homicide at the Ramada Inn downtown."

"Okay, Detective Townes, we are on our way. I'll inform the medical examiner's office."

"Thanks." Zack hung up and slipped his cell back in his pocket.

Kim said, "All right, he's been Tasered. That's a given. That probably led to a heart attack. He falls in the pool and drowns."

"That's plausible." Zack stood up and looked around for any surveillance cameras.

Bingo!

"Better yet, we might have proof. Look at those cameras mounted over there on the poles."

They briskly headed for the front desk to speak to the Indian manager. He was slim and six feet tall. He was attired in his traditional garb.

After introducing himself and showing his badge, Zack asked, "I noticed two cameras are mounted near the pool. Can we have a look at them?"

"Sure."

In the video, the victim was talking with someone under the awning adjacent to the pool. The footage was a side view of the pudgy victim, but the person he was talking to was standing behind a cement pillar. He seemed upset as he threw his hands in the air and pointed his finger toward the person he was talking to. Suddenly, bolts of light flashed, zapping him in the face and neck area. The victim stumbled backward toward the pool while grabbing his chest. He fell into the water. He kicked a few times. Then his body sank to the bottom, and several minutes later, he floated to the top.

They all watched in amazement. Zack frowned. The killer seemed aware of the cameras, angling his or her body behind that pillar for as much cover as possible. "Is there any way we can zoom in the screen to get a better look at that killer?"

"I'm going to need this tape as evidence," Zack told the manager.

"Okay. No problem." The manager hit the stop button, ejected it, and handed it over.

"Now," Zack said, "we need to check out his hotel room."

The manager led them to the victim's hotel room, opened it, and waited outside. Once inside, the cops noticed the whips, chains, and spiked collars.

"Damn, this looks like some S&M shit," Zack said.

"You got that right." Kim cursorily looked at the twenties and hundreds scattered on the floor amid a driver's license that had Sam Walker stenciled on it. "Well, robbery doesn't seem like the motive here."

They looked at each other. They both knew, but neither one wanted to say it. Their serial killer had struck again. With the bodies piling up and the leads short, Zack hoped the new murder weapon they had found at the Tuck scene would give them something—anything—to go on.

Chapter 40

The forensics team was able to lift a perfect fingerprint from the knife that Kim and Zack had found at the Tuck crime scene. Agent Tally had vowed she would use every resource at her disposal to solve these murders, so in no time, she ran the prints, with Zack and Kim at her side, through AFIS. And she got a hit right off the bat. A photo of Jose DeJesus appeared on the screen. He was from El Paso, Texas.

Zack kept studying his picture. "He looks familiar. I believe he's the guy at the tattoo shop that's on the wall that was flashing gang signs with two other guys. I should have them on my cell phone." Zack whipped out his cell. He scrolled down a list of pictures, found the one he was looking for, and touched the screen to make it larger. And then he showed it to Becky and Kim.

They leaned in. "That's him," they both said at the same time.

"So, that makes sense." Becky said. "The names Zeta and Sinola are familiar Mexican cartels."

"I know personally," Zack said. "I went out to El Paso and then to Juarez, Mexico. And almost got killed several weeks back."

"But where is he now?" Kim asked.

"Hopefully, he's still in Tilton," Zack replied.

A nosy junior officer strolled by their cubicle and wondered what all the talk was about. He stopped in to see. He glanced at the picture and nonchalantly said, "Oh, that dude." He pointed. "I arrested him yesterday for DUI and a few other charges."

Zack's eyes lit up. "What!"

"Yeah, Detective. I got him for DUI, revoked driver's license, and expired tags. He was driving a new Escalade."

Zack hugged him. "Thanks, man."

Becky asked, "Where is he now?"

"In a holding cell, waiting to be processed."

They all hurried over there to see him.

Jose was disheveled. His hair was messed up, his clothes were rumpled, and he appeared to be suffering from a hangover. He slowly stared back at them.

"This is cause for a celebration," Zack said. "But I'd like to call for an impromptu press conference. That's after I clear everything with Chief Watts and the powers-that-be first."

That evening, Zack, Kim, and Becky were sitting at a table as they fielded questions from the media. They felt upbeat as they were grilled about finding Mr. Tuck's killer. And they didn't know at the moment if Jose had committed the other murders, but they would leave no stone unturned in finding out. But things turned sour as a male reporter asked Zack about his missing daughter.

Zack's expression changed suddenly. A tinge of emotion swept across his face. His bottom jaw quivered.

Kim saw what was happening and jumped in and said sternly, "This press conference is not about a missing child but rather about finding the killer."

"That's right." Becky chimed in.

"It's over. That's it." Kim waved off the other questions.

Kim got up, walked over, and hugged Zack. "You okay, hon?"

"Yeah, yeah." He stared at the media types that were dispersing. "I'll be all right."

Becky came over and patted him on the back as he got up to leave.

They chose a popular bar and grill in an upscale section of town. It was Friday, it had been a long week, and they wanted to let off a little steam. Becky and Kim really hit it off, especially after a few drinks. They laughed and chatted as Zack decided he was going to get wasted. He drank four Zombies and three Long Island iced teas. His speech was slurred.

Kim felt comfortable telling her new friend that he had been drinking and smoking quite heavily since Kathy left. Zack sat in their booth and dozed off from time to time.

Becky and Kim had another round as they talked like best friends. Then, Becky asked Kim if she and Zack would mind spending the weekend with her at her home. She got really lonely because her husband was gone all the time. And it was just a little over thirty minutes away.

Kim said all right after she called and cleared everything with Mrs. Jane. She was watching the boys. After helping Zack to the vehicle, they were on their way.

The next morning, they got a look at Becky's spacious home, and a barking white Maltese met them.

Becky picked him up. "Rocky! Rocky! How's my boy?"

"Do you have an aspirin, Becky?" Zack asked. "Hangover, I guess."

"Sure, there's a bottle on the counter."

Zack popped a few in his mouth and drank a glass of water. Kim and Zack looked at each other and thought about Fluffy, their female Maltese. After they stroked his coat to calm him down, Rocky went to check out the newcomers. He stopped and growled before he began to smell them.

"Isn't it ironic that we have a female Maltese just like Mr. Rocky here?" Kim gazed down at Rocky.

As Kim and Zack made their way around the home, they were amazed at how nice and huge it was.

"Wow! The FBI must be paying some good money these days," Zack said.

"I wish," Becky replied. "I do get paid a decent salary, but not the type of money that would allow me to live here. My husband, Eric, is a hedge fund manager."

"Okay, that's says it all," Kim said.

"Eric stays in New York. He comes home twice a month on one of his friend's private planes."

At the moment, all three and Rocky were leaving the foyer as they strolled down the main hallway, heading for the back of the house. A bright sun met them as they walked onto the deck. At the end of it was an Olympic-sized swimming pool.

"Do you want to have a few drinks by the pool?"

"Yes," Kim said. "We would love that."

A few hours later, they were eating hamburgers and drinking Heinekens while listening to Becky's eclectic playlist of music. Becky had asked what type of music they liked, and they had said, "anything." So music from Beethoven, the Eagles, Marvin Gaye, and country music like the Judds came from the Bose player.

Zack dove into the warm pool. He swam for twenty minutes, climbed out, stretched out into the lounge chair and sipped his Heineken. He then began to brood about Kathy. Maybe she left the area and took up with her boyfriend. But she never mentioned a boyfriend. Then another thought came to his mind. Perhaps an older man liked her, and they ran away together. He shook his head as if to erase those thoughts from his mind. Next, he reached for the pack of Newports on the glass table. Several feet away, Becky and Kim were grilling. A small shawl wrapped around their hips covered their bikinis.

"Hey, Becky," Zack hollered, "mind if I smoke?"

She looked over at him. "Go right ahead. I don't mind."

He lit up the Newport and finished his third Heineken. "Kim, can you bring me another beer?"

Becky took off her shawl. The red bikini she wore looked like it was painted on her. She had an hourglass body, a perfect round butt that the bikini tried to hold in. But some of those cheeks just hung out. Zack glanced away, feeling embarrassed and a bit guilty.

"Here you are, hon." Kim held a plate with a hot dog, hamburger, and Heineken.

"Thanks, Kim," Zack said.

They hung around the pool for several more hours swimming, eating, drinking, and listening to the tunes. Then Becky asked Kim to follow her into the house. She wanted to ask her a few questions about Zack's daughter.

They put their shawls back on and went into the patio.

Becky asked, "What do you think about his daughter? Did you guys get along?"

"No, not at all. She basically hated my guts from the start."

"Why? Did you do anything to her?"

"No, I guess it's the stepmother thing."

"I get it," Becky said. "Have you guys contacted Missing and Exploited Children?"

"No," Kim said, "this situation is a little different. Kathy left on her own. She wrote a Dear John letter pretty much saying she wanted to live her lifestyle and be left alone."

"What lifestyle might that be?"

"Prostitution."

"Seriously?"

"That's why I believe Zack is so disappointed in her. She wasn't raised like that."

"Wow," Becky said. "I would have thought drugs."

"Those, too." Kim added.

They talked a while longer, and then the conversation changed.

Kim asked as she looked around, "Where's your maid? Everything is so neat and orderly."

"It's me. I'm the maid."

"No way."

"It's not that hard. Rocky's our only kid."

At the sound of his name, Rocky got up, barked once, turned in a circle, and plopped back down.

"Even so, you have a career. How do you manage?"

"Lots of late nights and elbow grease. I guess you can say I'm a bit of a neat freak."

It sounded more like an OCD, but Kim kept that to herself.

Becky steered the conversation back to Zack. "You think hanging out helped Zack?"

"I hope so. Thanks for having us over."

They hugged. And when they were back at the pool, Zack was bobbing his head and singing along with the Commodores hit, "Brick House."

Chapter 41

In order to warm up the crowd at the strip club in the early hours, Nasty had what he called open mic. It was a way that local aspiring talent could get exposure like rappers, singers, and dancers. Just about any act could participate. The only requirement was that you had to be at least twenty-one years old. Each winner got a hundred bucks. Ever since his debut, Rat, Nasty's sidekick, had won convincingly.

At the moment, he was about to perform. The club was dark except for a big spotlight that lit up the catwalk. The DJ was playing Michael Jackson's "Billie Jean." Rat stepped out of the dark into the light. He was dressed in Michael's costume from the video, even the glittering shoes. He moonwalked from the catwalk to the edge of the stage next to the stripper pole. Patrons smiled with appreciation and clapped loudly. He went into his routine like Michael Jackson. He kicked up his legs and gyrated his hips. For the duration of the song, he was spot-on, hitting every move. And when he finally finished, the tipsy crowd gave him a standing ovation, even Nasty who was impressed and sitting at the bar.

Winded and sweating heavily, Rat made his way from the stage and through the crowd, getting pats on the back as he headed toward Nasty.

"What do you think, boss?

Nasty picked him up and placed him on the apron of the bar. "Rat, my man, you missed your calling. Michael Jackson couldn't have done it any better."

"Thanks, Nasty." Rat wiped sweat from his brow. "Damn, I'm thirsty. I need a drink."

Nasty said, "Little man, you know you can't hold your liquor."

A few days earlier, Rat had drunk a half pint of Jack Daniels and gotten so out of hand, cussing out Nasty and others of their clique, that his boss thought about putting him in the Rat Cage, a cage he had kept after the death of his beloved parrot he owned for many years.

"Just a beer, Nasty. A single beer, man. I'll behave," Rat said.

"All right."

Nasty waved the bartender over. "Give him a Coors Light. That should be okay for him."

"Hell, that's piss water. It won't give me a buzz."

Nasty laughed. "It should make your little ass drunk."

The bartender slammed the mug on the bar, wasting some. "That mug is half as big as you."

Rat rolled his eyes, grabbed the frosty mug with both hands, turned up the brew, and had a drink. And when he brought it back down from his long mouth, suds dripped from his whiskers, or mustache as he liked to call it.

"Oh, yeah," he said, smacking his lips, "the refreshing taste of beer to quench my thirst."

By now, it was ten thirty at night. People were filing into Naughty Women. At the moment, women got in free before eleven. And any drink under five dollars was free, courtesy of the house. Nasty always knew, where there were women, the men would come. He owned other strip joints, but Naughty was his pride and joy. He had placed a lot of time and money in it. And finally, it had started turning him a hefty profit, in addition to his escort service.

"We had enough fun tonight." Nasty turned serious. "We got some business to attend to tomorrow night. Y'all come to my office. I've got something I've been working on," he said to his crew who were only a few feet from him, sitting at a couple of tables.

His grand plan was to rob Mexican cartel leader Jose DeJesus and his Zeta boys that he had done business with in the past. This happened a week before Jose was arrested for a DUI. The meeting was set out in the county in an open field.

Both sides, the Mexicans and Nasty's crew, were armed to the teeth with all types of assault weapons like AR-15s, TEC-9s, AK-47s, and Uzis. Business was being conducted out in a dark clearing in front of the headlights. Rat was wearing all black and a ski mask. He had snuck out of the side door of Nasty's car. The plan was, the time the drug money was shown, someone from Nasty's camp would be in the woods with a bullhorn, pretending to be the cops on a stakeout, distracting the drug transaction. And while the Mexicans' attention would be placed on the man in the woods, Rat would steal the briefcase of money.

Everything went off without a hitch. Rat was gone in seconds. He had reappeared back in Nasty's floorboard, laughing his ass off as he tightly held to the briefcase.

Once the Mexicans realized they had been hoodwinked, all hell broke loose. Gunfire came from everywhere. Many of the combatants took cover as they fired their weapons. And when the shooting stopped, screams of pain and moans were heard in the night air. Vehicles were started. Engines revved, and tires screeched into the night.

"Yeah! Yeah!" Nasty screamed. "We got them. I bet they'll know better the next damn time."

Miraculously, Nasty wasn't hit in the hail of bullets. He once stole a glance and realized Rat had the briefcase of money. He slowly wobbled to the back of his car and lay on the ground until the shooting was over. He sensed things would turn out the way it did. A few of his men were hit though, one in the shoulder and the other in the hand.

Nasty checked them out and figured they basically had superficial injuries. "That ain't nothing. Nothing an aspirin and a few stitches can't fix. Carry y'all's asses to hospital and get some help." He patted them on the backs. "Now, where's that damn Rat? I need my money."

Rat was still in the floorboard. "Right here, Boss." He stood up and looked out the side window.

"You got my money?"

"Yes, it's right here."

"Lemme see it."

Rat crawled out the back with the briefcase in tow. Nasty grabbed it, went to the headlights of his car, and popped the lid. His eyes lit up. Then he inhaled the stacks of greenbacks. "Nothing like the smell of money."

Suddenly, everybody froze. Off in the distance, they could hear the wailing of police sirens.

"Hey," Nasty said with his eyes bucked, "somebody must have called the cops. Let's get the hell out of here."

Rat darted for the passenger side of Nasty's car, and the rest of his crew scrambled toward their vehicles as Nasty wobbled as fast as he could for his car door. He turned on the engine and disappeared into the night.

Chapter 42

Once Zack got word of the shooting and the wounded at the hospital, he rushed out of his cubicle, exited the building, and jumped in his car. He was up at the hospital in record time.

Among the injured were two of Nasty's men, and one Mexican was a Zeta. Zack told the physician on duty in the ER not to let any of them leave until he had interviewed them. He said okay.

Zack pulled back the curtains and stepped inside the small room. When he initially saw them, they were writhing in pain. There were two guys. One was in his late teens, maybe early twenties, named Rontae. He massaged a bandaged shoulder. The other was a skinny guy in his midtwenties, Slim, with bandages on his right hand.

"I'm Detective Townes," Zack said. "What happened last night?"

They just stared up at him without saying a word. Zack wasn't surprised. There was a street code that he was all too familiar with over the years. Never rat or snitch someone out, even if that person nearly took your own life. He had seen it so many times while interviewing these so-called street thugs.

A minute passed. There was still silence. The two grimaced with their eyes downcast, holding on to their injuries.

Zack finally spoke. "I know what you guys were up to tonight. I've been around a long time. Those Mexicans you guys had a shootout with are not playing."

Their gaze traveled from the floor up to the big detective.

"I just got back from Texas and Mexico, and believe me, they will wipe y'all off the map. The beheading a few months back, that was them. So unless you look forward to the coroner bagging and tagging you in separate pieces, I suggest y'all better start talking."

They looked at each other. Zack's little speech seemed to be setting in.

Rontae hesitantly spoke up, stammering. "I ... I ... I did what I was told."

Zack said, "And what was that?"

Rontae nervously looked over at Slim. His partner shrugged. "Go ahead and tell him."

"We were going to rob them Mexicans."

Zack cut him off. "We? Who are we?"

They exchanged glances.

Slim said, "Hell, don't look at me. Tell the cop."

"Big Nasty," Rontae said. "I'm sure you heard of him."

The fat pig at the strip club.

"Yes, the name rings a bell."

Rontae told Zack about the robbery.

"That was dumb," Zack said.

"Well, that's what went down."

"So, I gather this was Nasty's great plan. Now where is his fat ass?" Zack asked.

Slim said, "He's probably somewhere laughing and counting his money."

Zack had a thought. He waited for a moment before springing it on them. "Just suppose I want to take down Nasty. Are you guys willing to testify against him?"

"Hell naw!" they said in unison.

"Man, Nasty is mean and crazy." Rontae added. "No, no, sir. I've seen him hit a guy in his chest and stop his heart for 'bout ten seconds."

Zack chuckled. "Nasty's got you boys running scared."

Rontae said, "I ain't shamed. You damn right. I've learned not to cross him too often."

Zack laughed. "What about the information y'all gave me? I think he wouldn't like that."

Slim cast a harsh look at Rontae. "I didn't say anything."

Rontae stared back. "Me either."

"Just think about it, fellas. Unless you play ball, I can't protect you from Nasty."

As Zack left the room, the ER doctor stopped him and breathlessly said, "Hey, have you heard what happened?"

"No, what?"

"That Mexican that was shot; he slipped out of the hospital."

"Damn!" Zack said. "So, I guess his injuries weren't that bad then."

"No. He was shot in the forearm. I gave him a shot for pain. He's lucky the bullet missed the bone and many arteries and veins."

"Thanks anyway, Doc."

Chapter 43

Nasty decided he would take some of his boys out to eat at a Mexican restaurant after his big drug deal. He loved Mexican food, in part because it was spicy. But Rontae was suspiciously not with them.

Quite a few were around Tilton. He chose Amigos. It was downtown, adjacent to the business district. They all piled out of their vehicles and headed for the front entrance. Slightly winded, Nasty stopped to get his breath.

"Y'all go on in." He held the front door of Amigos as they filed in.

It finally dawned on him. Rontae wasn't with them. "Where's Rontae?"

They turned around and shrugged their shoulders.

"You okay, boss?" Rat took up the rear as he stared up at him.

"Yeah, yeah. I'll be all right,"

The waitress, a young Hispanic woman in a gray uniform, led them to a big long table in the middle of the restaurant. It was three in the afternoon. The place was nearly empty.

After everyone was seated, their boss finally made his way over to the table. He flopped down in an empty chair at the head of the table.

"Did anybody bring my Beano?" Nasty asked breathlessly.

His longtime lackeys, Slim and Tyrone, looked at each other and then shrugged.

"Naw, we must have forgot, Nasty," Slim said.

"Y'all know I gots to have my Beano when I eat Mexican food."

"What's with the Beano?" Rat asked as his little, short legs dangled from his chair that seemed to swallow him up.

"I git a little gas when I eat this shit." Nasty chuckled. "But I love the food though. Can't get enough of it."

"Just give me the keys to the ride, boss," Rat said playfully. "I'll run down to the store and buy you a few bottles of um …"

Nasty and a couple of his men laughed.

"Quit sucking up to Nasty." Slim massaged his bandaged hand a few times.

"What!" Rat's tone switched.

The waitress brought them all a menu apiece.

"You lucky the waitress came. 'Cause I was about to let you have it," Rat said.

Within five minutes, they all had placed their orders. The waitress took up the menus and left.

Slim continued messing with Rat. "I wonder if Amigos got a high chair to put your little ass in so you can eat."

Another round of laughs ensued.

"You aren't funny, punk!" Rat stood up in his chair and pointed his finger across the table at Slim. "Don't make me bust a cap in your ass."

Things were about to get out of hand.

"Children, children," Nasty said, defusing the situation. "Y'all just need to chill. We ain't the only ones in the restaurant."

"It's aren't, Nasty," Rat said. "Not ain't."

"Well, excuse me, Mr. English Teacher." Nasty looked at him sideways. "Okay, aren't."

By now, the waitress was back, passing out their plates of food from a small cart on wheels.

With his plate overflowing with food, Nasty rubbed his hands, staring at refried beans, burritos, tortillas, dirty rice, and a double portion of everything. And to top it all off, jalapeño peppers were mixed throughout his meal. Nasty was fond of saying of Mexican cuisine, if it didn't make your mouth and insides burn, it wasn't worth paying for.

"I'm starving, y'all. Let's dig in." Nasty got his knife and fork.

Their beverages of choice were Coronas and tequilas. They pigged out for the next forty-five minutes. Nasty left a twenty-dollar tip and thanked the waitress, and he followed his men out the exit. He rubbed his big, bloated belly before squeezing behind the wheel. Rat jumped in on the passenger side.

Nasty laughed, exposing his gap teeth. "I bet you I gained ten pounds today."

"You look nine months pregnant, boss." Rat laughed at this own joke. "When are you going to have those triplets?"

"You is a little, smartass bastard, ain't you?" Nasty backed out the parking lot and onto the highway.

"Here we go again." Rat basically ignored his boss's last statement. "It's you are. And it's not ain't, but aren't."

"Hey! Hey!" Nasty hollered. "Who's paying your dwarf ass?"

"You."

"Who just bought your meal?"

"You."

"So it's in your best interest to shut the hell up 'bout my talking, Rat. Do I make myself clear?"

Rat lowered his head. "Yeah, boss."

An awkward silence lasted until they got home.

Slim and the other guys had already arrived at Nasty's place. They sat in the vehicle, waiting for them. Nasty always kept his boys around him 24-7. They stayed armed to the teeth. In the drug dealing game, anything could jump off at any time.

Nasty yawned and rubbed his belly. "My stomach is feeling funny. Bubbling too much."

Tyrone said, "Boss, you got Beano in the house. I believe it's in the cabinet."

"Thank goodness." Nasty wobbled through the front door. He fetched the bottle and quickly popped three pills into his mouth. "Hey, fellows, I think I need a nap."

Nasty always wanted his team around even when he slept. He was that controlling. But for the most part, they didn't complain. They respected him, or was it fear? It didn't matter to Nasty. It was all the same.

———◦◦◦———

Rat took all this in. He was the latest addition to the group, so everything was new to him, like the close security he was witness to as their boss slept. Nasty was laying on the huge bed in the master bedroom. Slim, Tyrone, and the rest were relaxing in chairs and recliners around the room. The sunken mattress almost touched the floor as the big man tried to sleep.

"Hell, this is not going to work." Nasty grabbed a pillow as he went to the end of the bed and lay down on the hardwood floor. "Now, this is more like it." He squirmed a bit until he felt comfortable.

Resembling a big hog who had devoured a trough of food, Nasty began to fall into a deep sleep. He then began to snore really loudly.

Standing directly behind him, Rat started to imitate his boss from his snoring, the wobbling gait, and the gap teeth.

The crew snickered at Rat's antics. Then one of them got up and eased open a window. Rat wondered why he did that. It was nice and cool in the house. So as he kept on with his antics of Nasty. Moments later, he knew why the window was open. Nasty had passed gas. The Beano finally kicked in. The force and odor coming from Nasty's ass damn near knocked him to the floor.

"Goddamn! What the hell is going on?" Rat held his pointed nose. "A damn shit storm has broken loose. I need a gas mask."

The crew put their hands over their mouths, and they were crying as they laughed.

Rat looked like a version of Dorothy in *The Wizard of Oz* as he fought to stand through the fart tornado. And Nasty didn't let up as he snored and passed gas for nearly three minutes straight. And when he finally finished, an exhausted Rat crawled to the window, gulping in as much fresh air as his lungs could take.

"You guys knew he was going to do to that."

They all nodded in unison.

Chapter 44

Maria was in her apartment, lying on her bed and beginning to recall how her life had become so topsy-turvy over the last couple months. Once she had escaped a mental facility back in El Paso, she changed her birth name from Maria Cortez to Caitlyn Cortez. She didn't have anything—clothes or money. She was completely broke. It was as if her life were put on hold for eight years there. She really didn't know anyone in El Paso other than her landlord.

She thumbed and got a ride to the rundown apartment complex she grew up in. After she thanked the driver, he pulled off in a cloud of dust. Maria was blinded as the cloud disappeared and the horror was before her. Almost paralyzed with fear, she stood frozen in her tracks. A cold chill swept over her body even though it was hot as hell out in the Texas sun. Staring at the building, she managed to slowly put one foot in front of the other, tentatively making her way past a group of young kids playing kickball in the courtyard.

With the greatest reluctance, she went up the small, rickety, wooden stairs and onto the porch. She walked another twenty feet and peered through the open curtains where she once lived. A flood of memories ran through her mind, like the constant beatings she got for the simplest things, such as asking for something to eat when she was hungry or crying because her soiled diaper needed changing.

And there was the verbal abuse. Her mother would scream at her from the top of her lungs. All of that was terrible enough, but the worse thing she would never get over was the rapes. They were brutal, relentless, and forever etched into her mind. The only solution, the only way to put those demons to rest, was to get those bastards back by any means necessary. There were several of them, but three stood out because they came back, repeatedly raping her.

She was startled when someone inside the apartment came to the window.

Maria jumped. "Oh, I'm sorry. My mind was somewhere else."

An old, scrawny white man with a bald head waved for her to come in. Then he went and opened the front door. "Would you like to come in? To get a better look."

"No, no, mister." She threw up her hand. "I was just thinking about the time when I grew up here." There was a short silence. "Hey, mister, can you tell me who the landlord is, if you don't mind?"

He scratched his baldhead, thinking. "Yeah, that be Mrs. Jennifer Santos."

A big smile crept across Maria's face. "Thank you, sir." She shook his hand.

She happily strolled around back to the manager's office. An old, faded Celica was parked in the manager's space. Maria realized that was her ride.

When she walked in the office, Mrs. Santos was on the other side of the counter with her back turned as she was typing something on the computer.

Disguising her voice like a man, Maria said, "I need some plumbing done at my apartment."

"Just a minute, sir," Santos said without turning around. "I'll be right with you."

Laughing to herself, Maria said, "No, I need it done right now."

The landlady suddenly turned around. She studied a smiling Maria for a few moments. Then her face lit up when she recognized her. Tears of joy ran down her dry cheeks. "I can't believe it. I can't believe it. Maria! Maria!" She jumped up and came from around the counter, and they embraced for three straight minutes. "Girl, I thought you were dead."

"Hell, I thought I was dead, too. Only by the grace of God am I still here."

"Where have you been?" Santos asked.

With her face clouding up, Maria said, "I'd rather not talk about it."

"I understand," Santos replied, rubbing her hands, "but you are still alive."

Changing the topic, Maria asked, "How's your family?"

Santos sighed. "Well, my husband died of a massive heart attack. My only child, Anne, got married and moved to Washington."

Being on the run, Maria needed some money and wheels. She didn't want to seem desperate, but she was. "Mrs. Santos, I know this sounds strange, but I need a little help. Money and a vehicle. You know—"

Santos cut her off. "I always thought of you as a daughter. I know the situation you had with your mother was horrible. I felt your pain. So I made myself a promise. If we ever met again, I'd help you out."

"So, you'll do it?"

"Absolutely."

Maria hugged her. "Thank you so much, Mrs. Santos."

"Hold on, Maria."

Santos left for a minute and came back with a set of keys and a small stack of money.

"Here are the keys to the Celica."

"What are you going to drive?"

"See that car with that cover over it." She pointed across the parking lot. "I drive that on special occasions. The old car was for running little errands around town. But here's four hundred dollars. Hopefully it will help you."

"Yes, yes indeed. Thank you so much."

They embraced for the last time. Santos stood in the doorway as Maria unlocked the Celica.

Maria smiled. "So how many miles does the car have?"

"Over a half million," Santos said proudly. "But she's on her last legs. I hope she holds."

"I think she will. Bye. Thanks again."

<hr />

Maria drove to his job and parked. The shift was about to end. She waited patiently as she filed her nails. It had been eight years since she'd last seen him. After asking a few people, she found out where he worked. She parked next to the exit ramp to make sure she didn't miss him. Beside her was her purse. She stopped filing her nails, opened her purse, and checked for the second time to see if her straight razor and .380 were still there.

The shift bell sounded. Her heartbeat went up a few paces. Then her gaze fell on the mass of people almost running out of the building. Her eyes were focused on everybody coming down the ramp, searching for Byron Stumbs, the child rapist, one of her tormentors.

And when she spotted him, she could hear her heartbeat in her ears. Byron had gained a lot of weight, and he was wearing a beard. He walked briskly past her car. She blew her horn. He stopped and stared at her. He was puzzled for a second as he tried to place the face.

He smiled as he recognized her face. "Maria! Maria!" He rushed to the driver's side. "Long time no see. You've turned into a beautiful young lady."

"Thanks."

There was an awkward silence.

"So, what are you doing now?" he asked.

"Nothing really."

"Want to hang out for old times' sakes?" Byron asked.

"Sure. Why not?"

"Okay, follow me to my place. I have a trailer out in the country."

"All right."

The drive took twenty minutes. Maria had decided she would make the killing quick. She pulled right behind his black Ford pickup. They got out of their vehicles and headed for the trailer.

"I can't believe how beautiful you turned out," he said, "but you were always pretty as a young girl."

They went inside. His statement pissed her off. Anger coursed through her veins. She already had the .380 trained on the back of his head.

When Byron turned around after retrieving two Buds from the fridge, his eyes were big as saucers. "Hey, what's going on, Maria?" he screamed.

"You sorry dog," Maria said, "you raped that pretty little girl. Remember! Where are the other two bastards that helped you?"

Byron dropped the bottles. They exploded on the floor, spewing foamy suds everywhere. "Please, don't shoot me. I don't know."

"Tell me!" Maria cocked the hammer. "I might let you live."

"Well, Ray Brownlow moved to his hometown, Tilton, Virginia. And Johnny Laws, he works at Tyson Furniture. He's a salesman."

Before he could utter another word, Maria unloaded the clip with eight rounds into his chest. When he crumpled to the floor, she stood over him and spat on his dying body. "Eight rounds for the eight times you raped me, you SOB."

The next morning, Maria was at Tyson Furniture at seven sharp. The parking lot in the back was nearly empty except for a green Accord. She watched Johnny as he got out of his car, unlocked the back door, and entered the building. The door didn't close completely. It was slightly ajar. Maria was thankful for that. She had left her gun in the car and brought her straight razor with her.

Johnny was busy flicking on the lights. He was startled when she stepped from behind a stanchion on the floor.

"May I help you, ma'am?" Johnny studied her for ten seconds. "Maria, is that you?"

"Yup." Her tone was flat. She didn't care for all the pleasantries. She just wanted to get the job done and leave.

"Wow. You're stunning."

"Is that right?" Maria had wanted to ambush him when he was unlocking the door, but she wanted him to see his face as she killed him.

He held out his arms. "Come, give me a hug."

She grit her teeth, mumbling, "This will be the last hug you will ever give," concealing the knife behind her back. And when he was within striking distance, she slit him across the neck, cutting his carotid artery as the blade came across the neck and chest at an angle.

Johnny reached for his neck. "What the hell?"

She struck him three times before he hit the shiny tiled floor. "I was a child!"

He was lying in a pool of blood, twitching a few times before dying. Maria wanted to get out of El Paso now, as quickly as possible. She needed to get to Virginia to get the last and worst bastard that violated her. But she noticed her engine light kept coming on. Damn, the last thing she wanted was to break down in the middle of nowhere.

Less than thirty minutes later, her nightmare came true. She had just made it halfway across Texas when steam was hissing from under the hood and a loud knocking sound followed. The Celica was losing power. She pulled onto the shoulder of the highway.

Maria screamed, "Aw shit!" She slammed her fists against the steering wheel.

It was at least a hundred degrees in the Texas sun. This stretch of I-10 was a desert that stretched for miles and miles. Nothing but barren earth, like a moonscape. Occasionally, a vehicle would whisk by.

Maria knew nothing about cars. She knew to just put gas in them when they were low and drive. She reluctantly climbed out and hoisted the hood. The steam wasn't as intense now as it spewed from a torn hole in the radiator hose. She peered around the engine and saw oil leaking from a fist-sized hole on the side.

She took a deep breath and sighed. She pulled her gaze from the car and looked out across the deathlike surroundings. A couple vultures were perched on a huge rock rutting from a hill.

Every so often, a vehicle would drive by, mostly tractor trailers headed eastbound. She had a choice: stay on I-10 and die, giving the vultures an easy meal or work her charm on the next vehicle going in her direction. So she went through her suitcase and found a skimpy red miniskirt, white blouse, and high heels. As she strutted down the road a few yards, the next semi driver slammed on his breaks as burning rubber filled the air.

"Damsel in distress," said a jovial, middle-aged black man, who was balding with a big gut, as he rolled down his window. "Must be my lucky day. Hop on in, and get out of that hot sun."

"Okay," Maria said happily. "I need to get my suitcase. I'll be right back."

"What's your name, cutie?

"Amy."

"Such a pretty name for a pretty young woman." His eyes dripped with lust as they traveled up and down her legs and thighs.

Perv.

"Thanks."

"So what happened to your car?"

She was a little relieved he changed the topic and kept his eyes on the road. "I don't know. I know absolutely nothing about cars. But it started messing up when the engine light came on. Then steam shot out from under the hood, and the next thing I knew, I heard a loud knocking noise. It lost power, and I pulled over on the side of the road."

He laughed. "I used to be a mechanic. It sounds to me like your thermostat probably got stuck. The engine got hot because water wasn't circulating around the block to cool it. Most likely caused it to crack or throw a rod."

"I also saw oil leaking from the engine."

"Yup, that's exactly what happened."

"Oh, you do know a lot about engines."

"Yup, but I'd like to know more about you, Angie."

"Amy," she said, correcting him.

Hell, she smiled on the inside. He could very well call her Angie or Amy. It wasn't her real name. But she did like the name Amy for the moment. In her purse, she kept a straight razor, .380, and even a Taser she hadn't used yet, just in case things got out of hand.

They made small talk for several hours. She occasionally allowed him to rub her thighs when he tried to fondle her as he drove. She resisted. Then she would grab his hand in a playful way and say "Naughty boy," all the while boiling with rage and suppressing the urge to cut his throat or hand. The throat would be quick and final. And if she cut his hand, he still could fight back. For now, she wanted to bide her time, especially getting past El Paso as far as she could.

"Yeah, my name's Tony by the way. I was married for several years. Have a boy and a girl, both grown. My daughter is around your age." There was a short pause. "I guess you're wondering why a dirty old man twice your age is hitting on you."

Right at that moment, she felt he spoke from the heart. And she kind of felt sorry for him and might let him live so long as he didn't try some funny shit, like trying to rape her. She laughed.

"Well, yeah, I'd be lying if I said that thought hadn't crossed my mind."

"But, you know, old or not, I'm still a man. I have needs."

She let out a nervous chuckle with a frown and then thought to herself, *Damn, the old bastard is no different than the rest of the men. He wants to take something that doesn't belong to him. He sees me as weak and vulnerable.*

"Let's change the topic," he said after reading her expression. "Want something to eat?

"Sure."

They had long passed by El Paso several hours earlier and were just a few miles from the Louisiana state line. Tony decided to stop at one of his favorite truck stops along his route, and when they made their entrance into the place, all eyes were on Maria. His fellow truckers stopped whatever they were doing, and a few whistled at the pretty young woman.

Tony beamed with pride. "What y'all think?"

Maria felt like a show pony. But she soaked up the attention. A few overweight waitresses scoffed with jealousy, and one remarked, "Hell, she ain't nothing but a prostitute out there on the highway selling her ass."

"Anything you want to eat, honey?" Tony said as they both scooted around a table in a wooden booth, sitting opposite of each other.

His elderly male friends couldn't finish their meals for gawking at Maria. One was so taken that he got up from his stool, walked over, and asked bluntly, "How'd you get her? I mean, where did you find her at?" He hovered over her now as she sat.

Flustered now, Tony snapped. "None of your damn business. Finish eating your damn food, and leave us the hell alone."

Somewhat embarrassed by all the attention now, Maria tucked her head slightly and stared at the table.

Tony asked, "You okay, hon? We can go somewhere else to grab a meal."

The guy turned on his heel, took a seat, and went back to eating his meal.

"No, everything is fine."

"A bunch of damn old geezers acting like they ain't used to seeing a beautiful young woman."

Nearing the Virginia and North Carolina line on I-95 and riding together for almost twenty-four hours and over fifteen hundred miles, Maria had gotten sick of Tony's advances. It was night now. She told him to pull off the highway and down a service road, and she would give him some. He obeyed. He turned down a remote road that had no streetlights and was almost taken over by weeds and parked.

"I've been waiting for this since I picked you up." He reached for her.

She fumbled for the .380 in her purse and got it. "Me, too. I couldn't wait to put a bullet between your damn eyes."

A single shot rang out through the nearby woods. Tony slumped over across the middle console. Maria grabbed her small suitcase and purse and disappeared into the night.

Chapter 45

The next day, Nasty was back in his office, chilling and shooting the breeze with Rat and his boys, except for Rontae, when Maria strode in. She was wearing the outfit that she was about to perform in that night. It was a cheerleader getup: a pink, skimpy, miniskirt; a white, low-cut blouse with the letter M on the front; red-and-white pumps; and a set of pom-poms. She wore her hair in two long ponytails.

"So, what do you think, boss?" She swirled around.

Everybody's eyes went got big and wide. Their jaws dropped, even Nasty's. It wasn't the first time they had seen a woman looking so fine, but it was the first time that they, Nasty's men, had seen Maria.

Rat, being the clown he was known for, jumped his little ass out of his seat, strolled over toward her, encircled her twice, stuck out his tongue, and wrapped it around his longish mouth as his eyes were glued to her body.

"You are one fine ass woman." He stared up at her. "If you just give me a chance, I will eat you alive. Once you go with a dwarf, sweetie, you never go back." He winked.

Maria looked down at him with an amused expression on her face. "With all those sharp little teeth? No, sir. You ain't going to give me a hysterectomy."

The whole room erupted into laughter.

Even Rat had to laugh. "That's a good one. That's a good one. You got me."

Once the laughing died down, she asked again, "What do you think, boss? Will I knock 'em dead tonight?" She spun around one last time.

"No doubt. Absolutely," Nasty said. "You are the baddest girl I got in the house. Go make that money, honey."

"Okay, Nasty."

Maria left. Then Nasty thought about the little conversation he and Maria had the other day. It was unusual in that he showed his gentler side. And when he did, she opened up a little about her past, but not too much though. She had been sexually abused as a youngster. And she needed counseling from a psychiatrist and psychologist at the place, she liked to call it, to get herself back together. And to her surprise, Nasty could relate. He too had been sexually abused as a child by his uncle, something he always kept to himself until now. She was the first person he ever revealed that story to, and in a strange, odd way, Maria felt a personal kinship with him in that they shared the unfortunate tragedies. She thanked him for that, especially being a big man who had this reputation of being mean and tough. And she appreciated the kindness with which he treated her. He had tapped into feelings she never felt in her whole life before.

"Nasty! Nasty!" Rat stood on his desk, waving his hands in front of his fat face. "Earth to Nasty, are we back to reality or what?"

Nasty shook his head, letting out a hearty laugh. "Sorry, fellows. Spaced out a minute."

"I can't blame you. That new girl will do it to you," Slim said.

"That she will," Nasty replied.

Moments later, Slim told Nasty and the boys about what Zack had said at the hospital. Nasty was stretched out in his recliner with his feet up.

"Yeah, boss. Officer Townes said them Mexicans are coming after us because we stole their money."

"What!" Nasty said in an angry, high-pitched voice. He tilted his big head forward as he brought the recliner upright. "Say that again. I know you ain't been talking to some damn cop. Spilling your guts. Telling all my business."

Slim threw up his hands. "Hold on. Hold on now." He stammered. "I ... I ... I didn't say anything. Rontae did all the talking. I was just listening to him when the cop visited us at the hospital."

"Is you clear about that?" Nasty asked.

Nasty stared at him. "So, it was that damn Rontae, huh?"

Beads of sweat appeared on Slim's brow. He wiped them off with the back of his sleeve. "Yup. It was him, boss. Not me."

"I'll get his puny ass when he gets back. I believe he was stealing some drugs from me anyway."

Slim let out a breath.

Rat jumped around, throwing punches in the air and egging him on. "That's right, boss. Beat his ass."

"And another thing," Nasty said, stalking around the room, "if those fuckin' Mexicans want a woe, they got a woe!"

"It's war," Rat said. "Not woe. War, man. That isn't hard to say, Nasty."

Nasty glared down at Rat. It looked like steam came out of Nasty's ears.

179

Rat cut his eyes up at him, swallowed hard, and managed to say, "Yikes!"

It was too late. Nasty snatched him up in one swipe of his hand by the throat, lifting him in the air. "I'm about sick of you, you damn rodent!" he said through his clenched gap teeth. "I will choke the life out of you."

Clawing at his hands and with his little feet kicking and eyes about to pop out, Rat was fighting for his life.

"Don't kill him, Nasty," someone from the crew said. "We like him. He makes us laugh."

Nasty released his grip. Rat fell to the floor. Then he looked hard at Nasty as he was getting his breath. Then he dragged himself over to the boys. Once he gathered himself, he mumbled, "A scattered tooth, illiterate swine."

The atmosphere was tense for an hour. Nasty settled into his recliner and dozed off for thirty minutes. Rat entertained the crew by imitating Nasty in the easy chair.

Suddenly, Nasty's cell phone rang.

"Where is you? Where is you, boy?" Nasty screamed into his cell phone.

"I'll be there in a few," Rontae said nervously. "I'm coming, boss."

A bit later, the doorbell rang. Nasty climbed out of his easy chair, wobbled toward the door, and opened it.

"There you is," Nasty said, taking up nearly all of the door frame. "You little snitch. Bring your narrow ass in here, boy."

Nasty grabbed Rontae by the collar and yanked him inside. He slammed the door. Nasty pointed his finger in Rontae's face. "I heard you like dropping dimes on people. I'm 'bout to drop some quarters on your punk ass, boy."

A surge of fear ran through Rontae's veins. "Let me explain myself, man."

Before he could utter another word, Nasty backhanded him. The blow burst Rontae's bottom lip, where blood began to flow out. Rat and the crew watched intently. They were spellbound.

With tears in his eyes, Rontae touched his bleeding lip and looked at his red fingertips. Suddenly, he ripped the 9 millimeter from his waistband. "Don't make me shoot, you big ass, motherfucker!" Rontae backed up as the gun shook in his hand and his knees knocked.

Nasty let out a devilish laugh, inching closer to him. "Boy, I'll make you eat that gun."

"Don't come any closer. I'll shoot! I'll lay your fat ass out!"

"Yeah, I bet," Nasty said. "Give me that gun, bitch." Nasty snatched the gun from his hand and commenced pistol-whipping him. "Didn't I tell you not to mess with Nasty. I ain't no joke. I bring the pain. I got that name for a reason, boy."

Rontae collapsed to the floor with blood coming from the cuts and gushes about his swelling head. The crew watched in awe, knowing full well the same could happen to them if they got on his bad side.

Nasty waved his hand. "Git him out of here, y'all. He disgusts me."

The crew moved toward Rontae.

"Hold up!" Rat reached into his pockets and brought out what appeared to be a pair of brass knuckles.

Lying on his back, Ronate dizzily looked up.

Rat rushed over and stood on his chest. "How you like some of my knuckle sandwich, punk?" Rat punched him in the face, knocking him out cold. "Just cleaning up your job, boss." Rat stepped off his chest and gave a dismissive wave. "You guys drag him out of our sight."

Chapter 46

The next day, Kim, Zack, and Becky were sitting at the conference table at the police station brainstorming about the four unsolved murders. Getting Walker's name took some work. He had over five aliases. But after some digging, Zack finally came up with his real name. The detective figured he probably used so many names because he was married and had a career as a stockbroker and didn't want to be found out.

Becky started. "Nearly all the men were white and middle-aged. They were either cheating on their wives or into kinky sex."

Zack said, "Becky, the commonalities you raised are striking. I was thinking the same thing."

"Yeah, the Walker guy killed at the Ramada Inn and all that S&M paraphernalia would suggest a female killer, a dominatrix type."

Kim asked, "But why would she stun him with a Taser?" She paused and answered her own question. "Well, unless they had an argument or fight. Perhaps he didn't want to be a slave anymore,"

"And as far as the Stewart and Cohen killings," Zack said, "let's say it's the same person, a female. She shot them and left them naked to prove a point. That she's in charge. To let them know she's the dominant one. That Kyle guy's penis was cut off, again showing dominance."

"Was there any evidence at the Ramada Inn?" Becky asked.

"Yes," Kim said.

"I haven't heard anything from the forensics team about the Walker case yet." Zack got up from the table and pulled out his phone. "Let me give them a ring right quick." He talked for two minutes and came back to the table. "At the Walker crime scene, they have a shoe print, flakes of skin, and a broken fingernail. Right now, they are casting a mold for the shoe print, and they have the skin and broken nail in solution, trying to extract a DNA sample from it."

Chapter 47

"Detective, I believe we've finally found her," said the uniformed cop on duty.

Zack blinked his sleepy eyes staring at the clock. It read 2:00 AM. He knew what the uniformed cop meant, but he didn't want to believe him. "Found who?"

"I think it's your daughter."

Zack's heart sank. He pushed himself upright against the headboard next to Kim. Being cops, they always slept lightly. The smallest thing always wakes one up. She heard the cop on the other end as well.

In a resigned tone, Zack let out a weary sigh. "All right. All right. Where?"

"At the Innkeeper."

There was only one Innkeeper in town. The fleabag motel was on the seedier side of Tilton. But it was one of the busiest places for prostitutes, pimps, and everyday criminal activity.

"I'll be there. Give me a few minutes."

"Okay, sir."

As he got dressed, a few tears rolled down his face. He slowly slipped on his trousers as he brooded about his little girl. It felt like an eternity as he buttoned his shirt and slipped on his shoes.

———◦———

When they arrived at the crime scene, several police cars were there, bathing the night blackness in a sea of blue as the lights on top of the cars blinked incessantly. Next to them were the CSI van, a medical examiner investigator car, and, much to his dismay, a satellite truck getting set up to run a live fed. They saw a pretty young brunette reporter under a floodlight going over her notes, rehearsing her line of questioning.

Zack barked, "Bastards."

"What, hon?"

"These bastards," Zack said as his anguish suddenly switched to anger. "How did these fucking media people get wind of it and beat us here?"

The story of the detective's missing daughter was plastered all over the local newspaper and media. The other killings seemed not to carry the same weight. It was something that never happened before in Tilton, and they were obviously intrigued. But now, everything had come to a head. She'd been found, and this made for a great lead story. News ratings would go up, and papers would fly off the shelves.

They got out of the patrol car. With renewed energy, Zack marched toward the blinking blue lights with Kim in tow. They ducked under the yellow police tape.

As soon as they did, a young female voice yelled, "Is the deceased your daughter, Detective Townes?'

Zack stopped in his tracks, sharply turned, and peered over his broad shoulders. He was about to say something, but Kim intervened.

"Don't know, miss!" Kim screamed in her direction. "If so, have a heart."

She nudged Zack in his back. They kept moving until they were inside.

A foul, stagnant odor hung in the air. As they made their way across the threadbare carpet and down a faded, peeling hallway, a group of police officers had gathered at an entrance to a room a few feet away. They hung their heads, and the huddle of cops slowly let the big man through with Kim right behind him.

Zack froze when he saw her. She was sprawled on an unmade bed with only her panties on. A flood of emotions washed over him. His bottom lip quivered, and beads of sweat began to pop out of every pore of his body, especially his baldhead.

"Oh my God! Oh my God!" he screamed. "My baby! My baby!" He rushed toward her.

"No! No!" The medical examiner investigator yelled. "Can't contaminate the crime scene."

Some of the largest members of the force were already there, just for this purpose. The big detective went berserk, throwing around two-hundred-pound men around like it wasn't anything. He let out a primal scream that was heard throughout the fleabag complex. It took six of them fifteen minutes to subdue him. He was then taken to the back stoop to calm down and get fresh air. The cops who took him back there were doubled over, trying to get their breath.

———⇒»●⇐———

Five days later, Kathy's funeral was held. It was a very hot day in late September. Black, ominous clouds spread across the sky. The threat of rain hung in the air. The funeral was held in a small white chapel built by the Townes family over one hundred and sixty years ago, at the time their forefathers were slaves.

The old church sat on a bluff overlooking a fast-moving creek, and clumps of oaks, birches, and maple trees surrounded it. Adjacent to it, no more than fifty feet away, was the Townes family cemetery. Three elderly gentlemen dressed in work clothes stood next to the freshly dug grave and gave a solemn nod as the procession of vehicles arrived at the entrance, led by a patrol car from the Tilton police department with a stretch limo directly behind it.

Dressed all in black, the Townes family and friends climbed out of the vehicles and slowly made their way into the chapel, filing in two at a time. Zack's huge body shook with sobs; he had taken off his tie and unbuttoned his collar. He was wearing his favorite Ray-Ban sunglasses. He dabbed at his eyes from time to time as Kim held tightly to his hand. His other two kids, Mrs. Jane, and Hosea followed behind them.

The organist played a very somber tune as the presiding pastor led the way, reading a passage from Ecclesiastes. Over half of the Tilton PD was there, from Chief Watts all the way down to the traffic cops. They sadly watched as the service proceeded. Sitting at the back of the church on the last pew was Becky. She hadn't known Zack or Kim all that long, but she had taken a liking to both of them. And for someone to lose a child so young, it would tear at anyone's heart. She felt tears welling up in her eyes.

For the next two hours, the church came alive as they gave young Kathy a joyous home-going. The choir sung their hearts out. A couple guest pastors gave inspirational sermons that ignited several old women to get up and to dance and shout. Even Mrs. Jane, Kathy's grandmother, stood up and gave her testimony.

As the service wrapped up, the mourners filed out into a brilliant sun that beamed high in the aqua sky. The dark clouds were gone now. Only a sea of blue let the warmth come from above.

The crowd then strolled over toward a black tent with Bryant's Funeral Home emblazoned on it. Underneath it was the freshly dug grave with ten folding chairs sitting on a green carpet. A mound of red dirt was next to the hole in the earth.

The presiding pastor gave out three red roses to the family members, and the casket was gingerly lowered into the ground. A few moments later, the patter of dirt could be heard hitting against the vault as the gravediggers went about their work. Somber members from the police department, most in uniform, patted Zack and Kim on their backs as they sympathized with their loss.

With tears in her eyes, Becky gave each a tight, warm, reassuring hug.

Chapter 48

Back at the station, Becky and Kim were hatching out a plan to get the culprit. After seeing how Mr. Walker was killed and finding S&M toys, Becky firmly believed the serial killer was a woman. She believed that the Tilton police department should put together a task force of different members, like SWAT, snipers, and other special unit members, and simultaneously bust the Naughty Women for allowing underage girls to strip and prostitute. That was where Skylar Hicks, their number-one suspect of the Stewart murder, worked. And out in the county, the Pruitt Farm was mixed up in it because Jose DeJesus was definitely involved in the killing of Tuck.

But they still didn't have the smoking gun from that murder yet.

Becky said, "Let's drop this dragnet on both places and see what we come up with."

But before any of her plans could be executed, she needed the approval of Chief Watts. He agreed and thought it was a brilliant idea. Also, they wanted the media personnel at both places running it live. They were on board as well.

The time was set for Saturday at ten in the evening, a very busy hour at the strip club. Everything would be in full swing, even at the Pruitt Farm, as the migrant workers were celebrating the weekend.

"Police! Police!" barked the cops in riot gear, wielding AR-15s and .40 calibers. "Hands up. Now!"

The DJ stopped playing music. Almost-naked strippers ran around screaming. Some tried to run out the back door. But it was already secured by several cops and a camera crew that took their pictures. Within an hour, Big Nasty, his strippers, including Maria, and his boys were filing out toward the paddy wagon in handcuffs.

Rat stuck out his tongue as he passed a camera. Nasty tried to kick and spit on a camera crew.

"What's the fucking charge, man?" Nasty asked a cop in all black.

"Didn't one of the officers read you your rights?" the cop asked.

"Yeah."

"You are charged with running a prostitution ring, especially with underage girls."

"That's a damn lie," Nasty said defiantly. "All them hos over eighteen."

"Whatever." The cop pushed him along.

Meanwhile at the Pruitt Farm, DeJesus's buddies were almost drunk when the raid went down. They laughed and spoke in Spanish as ten of them were loaded into a van with bars. Inside the modest home was a kilo of cocaine and two hundred pounds of marijuana. The media were all over the story as the confiscated drugs were spread across the ground under a floodlight.

Just behind the house was a shed. A member of the task force went to check it out. It was the black SUV the BOLO was out on months ago. He scoured the inside with his flashlight and located a secret compartment. He opened it and extracted a .25 pistol.

As the task force, Becky and Kim made their way back to the station to process the many people and drugs. They all gave each other high fives and fist bumps.

It took nearly six hours before everybody was booked from fingerprinting, mug shots, and other police procedures. Then the processing cops asked them if they would take a saliva swab. Everybody declined.

Once Becky learned of their refusal, she told the cops to offer them refreshments like gum, drinks, cigarettes, and things where they could get a DNA sample from. In no time flat, the department had their DNA and sent it to CODIS. After talking to a few high-ranking employees at CODIS, Becky was told the processing time would be from twelve to twenty-four days. She said she'd be waiting.

The two reporters from the media wrapped up their coverage, thanking the Tilton police for allowing them to come for the ride.

<hr>

At home the next morning, Kim was all giddy about what had happened the night before as Zack pulled himself from his self-imposed exile, reeking of alcohol, cigarette smoke, and body odor as he came through the door.

"Hon, we confiscated the twenty-five that we believe was used to help kill Mr. Tuck. They just need to get some DNA off it. We also found a kilo of cocaine and marijuana and took in a herd of those strippers." Her enthusiasm waned as Zack all but ignored her.

Suddenly, Zack's cell rang.

"Detective Townes, we got a name with semen found at the motel."

Zack quickly snapped out of his stupor. "What!"

Kim could hear the caller, too.

"Who is it? Who is it?" Zack demanded.

"Mr. Darnell Tomson."

"Tomson who owns the Lexus dealership."

"Yep. We double-checked ourselves because he seems like a stand-up guy. I had your department run a thorough background check on him. It seems he committed a sexual assault years ago. I guess he's been squeaky clean ever since. But—"

Zack cut him off. "Thanks." He slammed the phone in its cradle.

Kim knew that look. "Hold up, Zack."

"Hell no! I need to have a talk with him."

She tried to reason with him. She grabbed his arm. He snatched it away and stormed out the house.

Kim jumped on her cell and dialed Becky. "Where are you?"

"At the police station. Why? What's going on?"

"Some asshole, I believe from the medical examiner's office, told Zack that Darnell Tomson killed his daughter."

"Darnell Tomson?" Becky asked.

"Oh, I forgot. You aren't that familiar with Tilton. I tell you what. I'll pick you up, and we'll go down to the dealership."

"All right."

When they got there, Darnell had been thrown through a huge display window, and he was laying semiconscious in his torn suit amid shards of glass. Zack was making his way through the broken window to finish what he started.

Kim and Becky rushed out of the patrol car, screaming, "No! No, Zack!"

He looked in their direction, thought about what they were saying, and tamped down his rage. Zack grabbed Tomson's collar and leaned into his face. "You are one lucky SOB," he said through clenched teeth. He let Tomson go.

"I'm going to sue," Tomson managed to say.

"I don't give a shit," Zack replied, walking toward Kim and Becky.

They all jumped in the patrol car and headed for the police station. When they arrived, a seething Chief Watts and Dr. Powell waited for them outside the building.

"We need to talk, Detective." The chief was clearly straining to contain his anger.

"About what?" Zack asked.

Chief Watts shot back. "Your damn job."

Dr. Powell interceded, stopping Zack. "Detective Townes, whoever you called from my office didn't fully disclose my findings. I believe your daughter Kathy died from a seizure. There was Depakote, an anti-seizure medicine found in her tox report. I mentioned to your partner that her tongue didn't look right. The bite marks are consistent with a tonic-clonic seizure."

Zack was shocked. "What?"

"Your daughter died of a seizure. Mr. Tomson was not responsible."

Chief Watts cut his eyes sharply at Zack. "My office now."

Zack followed him down the hallway. The chief opened the door, let him in, and then slammed it shut. "Take a fucking seat, Zack. But before I proceed any further, give me your badge."

"All right." Zack reached into his pocket, got it, and flipped it onto this shiny desk.

The chief sighed. "Jesus, Zack. Look, I know she was your daughter, but there are a dozen videos of you on YouTube throwing an innocent man through a storefront window."

Dejected, Zack hung his head and slumped his shoulders. "But, Chief, I didn't know it at the time. Damn, have a heart. I thought he killed my daughter."

"You reek of booze, you smell like crap, and you haven't been to work in days. What am I supposed to do?"

Zack sat there with his shoulders slumped.

"I'm suspending you. Clean up your shit, and see a shrink. Then maybe we'll talk."

"What about the murders?"

"Tally and Patterson can handle it." Chief Watts waved his hand toward Zack. "You're no good to anyone like that."

Zack ground his teeth. There was nothing left he could say. Defeated, he stood slowly and shuffled out of the office. Becky and Kim were waiting in the hallway on a bench. They heard everything. They stood up when Zack came out.

"Give me a hug, hon." Kim extended her arms.

All three headed out of the building.

Chapter 49

Three weeks later, nearing the end of October, a snowstorm hit Tilton. And because of overcrowding and limited local funds, nearly everybody was released from prison except Big Nasty, DeJesus, and the drug dealers that possessed the kilo of cocaine and marijuana.

Maria was glad to get the hell out of the station. She vowed to never strip again but rather work through the escort service in order to get money. But the main objective for her being there was to get a hold of Ray Brownlow. A few days before the big bust at the strip club, she asked Blonde and a few other girls how often and what time he called the escort service. She listened and followed their instructions. It didn't take long before she made a connection. Maria disguised her voice a bit, and they agreed to meet at a Starbuck's parking lot at one in the afternoon. He said he would be driving a white Silverado truck. Just like clockwork, he was there on time.

Maria was waiting. She cut her engine off. She was wearing a blue hoodie. She threw the hood over her head, but before exiting the car, she grabbed a satchel and .380, stepping out into the thickly falling snow. She tapped on his passenger side window with her free hand. He unlocked the door. The engine was still running.

Mayor Brownlow stared over at her. "Pull back that hood so I can see you."

"Sure," she said. "Sure thing, Ray."

Maria slowly turned to face him, exposing the nasty scar he left on her. She pointed the gun at him.

"Maria!" he said breathlessly. "You're alive!"

She chuckled. "Alive and well, you bastard. Thought you got away with my murder, didn't you?"

He stammered. "I … I … I loved your mother. You know we go—"

"Shut the hell up!" she screamed. "Cut the damn crap. Follow my orders, and you will live a while longer."

"Okay," he said.

Maria climbed in the passenger seat. "Pull out of the parking lot. Go down the road a few blocks, and I'll tell you what to do next."

"All right."

The wipers were working feverishly, swiping the collecting snow from the windshield. The only sound was that of the wipers and the heater.

Maria pointed at a dilapidated two-story house. "See that rundown house?"

"Yeah."

"Pull in the yard." She never took the gun off him.

He pulled around back.

"Turn off the motor."

He did.

"Get out."

He went to say something, but she cut him off. "Shut the hell up! Get your ass out. Now!"

He opened his door and got out. She slid across the front seat on the driver's side behind him and grabbed her satchel as she went. As they headed for the back door, snow crunched under their feet as it kept coming down. And when they got inside, she demanded that he turn around with the .380 in her left hand and now a Taser in her right.

"Damn, are going to shoot or Taser me?"

"That's for me to decide, asshole."

She squeezed the Taser. Ray screamed and went down to one knee. She hit him again and again with the Taser. The jolts of electricity had him sprawled out. As he writhed in pain on the floor, he managed to say, "You bitch." He rolled onto all fours, trying to get up.

"Crawl to those stairs. Now!"

Ray slowly did what he was told. Once he finally got to the top of the stairs, Maria kicked him down the flight of stairs. She hustled down behind him. Ray tossed and turned in more pain.

"Get back on your knees, you dog, and crawl over to that damn iron bed."

"No! No, I am not—"

"Don't make me blow you brains out right this instant, Ray."

He trained his gaze up at her while on his back, turned on his side and then on all fours, and proceeded on his hands and knees toward the bed.

When Ray was a few feet from the bed, Maria screamed, "Get out of those clothes!"

"What?" he asked weakly.

"Do it."

A minute later, he was completely naked.

"Climb in that bed."

As he attempted to get in the rusty, metal bed, she shot him in the butt.

He hollered, grabbing his ass. "Bitch, you shot me in my ass!"

"That was my intention, you dog."

Then she zapped him several more times with the Taser until he was knocked out. And he woke up two hours later. His arms and legs were zip-tied to all four metal bedposts. Maria had pummeled him repeatedly with an iron pipe she had found on the floor while he was out.

As Ray barely clung to life, Maria stood at the bottom of the bed with the .380 trained on his forehead, between his eyes. "May you rest in hell, you fucking bastard."

The slug hit its intended target. Ray twitched twice and died. Just to make sure, she stepped closer and unloaded four more rounds into his skull.

The CODIS evidence implicated Maria. And when the cavalry—Becky, Kim, and others from the police department—showed up and surrounded the rickety house, Maria was so spent that she didn't resist but came out with her hands up. And she was promptly taken into custody.